The Magi And Other Selected Stories

Including the illustrated Essay 'A Note on Literature'

by

O. Henry

COMPASS CIRCLE

The Gift Of The Magi and Other Stories.
Current edition published by Compass Circle in 2022.

Published by Compass Circle

Note:
All efforts have been made to preserve original spellings and punctuation of the original edition which may include old-fashioned English spellings of words and archaic variants.

This book is a product of its time and does not reflect the same views on race, gender, sexuality, ethnicity, and interpersonal relations as it would if it were written today.

For information contact :
information@compass-circle.com

The true adventurer goes forth aimless and uncalculating to meet and greet unknown fate.

O. HENRY

SECRET WISDOM OF THE AGES SERIES

Life presents itself, it advances in a fast way. Life indeed never stops. It never stops until the end. The most diverse questions peek and fade in our minds. Sometimes we seek for answers. Sometimes we just let time go by.

The book you have now in your hands has been waiting to be discovered by you. This book may reveal the answers to some of your questions.

Books are friends. Friends who are always by your side and who can give you great ideas, advice or just comfort your soul.

A great book can make you see things in your soul that you have not yet discovered, make you see things in your soul that you were not aware of.

Great books can change your life for the better. They can make you understand fascinating theories, give you new ideas, inspire you to undertake new challenges or to walk along new paths.

Literature Classics like the one of *The Gift Of The Magi* are indeed a secret to many, but for those of us lucky enough to have discovered them, by one way or another, these books can enlighten us. They can open a wide range of possibilities to us. Because achieving greatness requires knowledge.

The series SECRET WISDOM OF THE AGES presented by Compass Circle try to bring you the great timeless masterpieces of literature, autobiographies and personal development,.

We welcome you to discover with us fascinating works by Nathaniel Hawthorne, Sir Arthur Conan Doyle, Edith Wharton, among others.

Contents

O. HENRY

Born	William Sydney Porter September 11, 1862 Greensboro, North Carolina
Died	June 5, 1910 New York, New York

O. Henry

THE GIFT OF THE MAGI AND OTHER STORIES

The Gift of the Magi

ONE dollar and eighty-seven cents. That was all. And sixty cents of it was in pennies. Pennies saved one and two at a time by bulldozing the grocer and the vegetable man and the butcher until one's cheeks burned with the silent imputation of parsimony that such close dealing implied. Three times Della counted it. One dollar and eighty-seven cents. And the next day would be Christmas.

There was clearly nothing to do but flop down on the shabby little couch and howl. So Della did it. Which instigates the moral reflection that life is made up of sobs, sniffles, and smiles, with sniffles predominating.

While the mistress of the home is gradually subsiding from the first stage to the second, take a look at the home. A furnished flat at $8 per week. It did not exactly beggar description, but it certainly had that word on the lookout for the mendicancy squad.

In the vestibule below was a letter-box into which no letter would go, and an electric button from which no mortal finger could coax a ring. Also appertaining thereunto was a card bearing the name "Mr. James Dillingham Young."

The "Dillingham" had been flung to the breeze during a former period of prosperity when its possessor was being paid $30 per week. Now, when the income was shrunk to $20, though, they were thinking seriously of contracting to a modest and unassuming D. But whenever Mr. James Dillingham Young came home and reached his flat above he was called "Jim" and greatly hugged by Mrs. James Dillingham Young, already introduced to you as Della. Which is all very good.

Della finished her cry and attended to her cheeks with the powder rag. She stood by the window and looked out dully at a gray cat walking a gray fence in a gray backyard. Tomorrow would be Christmas Day, and she had only $1.87 with which to buy Jim a present. She had been saving every penny she could for months, with this result. Twenty dollars a week doesn't go far. Expenses had been greater than she had calculated. They always are. Only $1.87 to buy a present for Jim. Her Jim. Many a happy hour she had spent planning for something nice for him. Something fine and rare and sterling—something just a little bit near to being worthy of the honor of being owned by Jim.

There was a pier glass between the windows of the room. Perhaps you have seen a pier glass in an $8 flat. A very thin and very agile person may, by observing his reflection in a rapid sequence of longitudinal strips, obtain a fairly accurate conception of his looks. Della, being slender, had mastered the art.

Suddenly she whirled from the window and stood before the glass. Her eyes were shining brilliantly, but her face had lost its color within twenty seconds. Rapidly she pulled down her hair and let it fall to its full length.

Now, there were two possessions of the James Dillingham Youngs in which they both took a mighty pride. One was Jim's gold watch that had been his father's and his grandfather's. The other was Della's hair. Had the queen of Sheba lived in the flat across the airshaft, Della would have let her hair hang out the window some day to dry just to depreciate Her Majesty's jewels and gifts. Had King Solomon been the janitor, with all his treasures piled up in the basement, Jim would have pulled out his watch every time he passed, just to see him pluck at his beard from envy.

So now Della's beautiful hair fell about her rippling and shining like a cascade of brown waters. It reached below her knee and made itself almost a garment for her. And then she did it up again nervously and quickly. Once she faltered for a minute and stood still while a tear or two splashed on the worn red carpet.

On went her old brown jacket; on went her old brown hat. With a whirl of skirts and with the brilliant sparkle still in her eyes, she fluttered out the door and down the stairs to the street.

Where she stopped the sign read: "Mme. Sofronie. Hair Goods of All Kinds." One flight up Della ran, and collected herself, panting. Madame, large, too white, chilly, hardly looked the "Sofronie."

"Will you buy my hair?" asked Della.

"I buy hair," said Madame. "Take yer hat off and let's have a sight at the looks of it."

Down rippled the brown cascade.

"Twenty dollars," said Madame, lifting the mass with a practised hand.

"Give it to me quick," said Della.

Oh, and the next two hours tripped by on rosy wings. Forget the hashed metaphor. She was ransacking the stores for Jim's present.

She found it at last. It surely had been made for Jim and no one else. There was no other like it in any of the stores, and she had turned all of them inside out. It was a platinum fob chain simple and chaste in design, properly proclaiming its value by substance alone and not by meretricious ornamentation—as all good things should do. It was even worthy of The Watch. As soon as she saw it she knew that it must be Jim's. It was like him. Quietness and value—the description applied to both. Twenty-one dollars they took from her for it, and she hurried home with the 87 cents. With that chain on his watch Jim might be properly anxious about the time in any company. Grand as the watch was, he sometimes looked at it on the sly on account of the old leather strap that he used in place of a chain.

When Della reached home her intoxication gave way a little to prudence and reason. She got out her curling irons and lighted the gas and went to work repairing the ravages made by generosity added to love. Which is always a tremendous task, dear friends—a mammoth task.

Within forty minutes her head was covered with tiny, close-lying curls that made her look wonderfully like a truant schoolboy. She looked at her reflection in the mirror long, carefully, and critically.

"If Jim doesn't kill me," she said to herself, "before he takes a second look at me, he'll say I look like a Coney Island chorus girl. But what could I do—oh! what could I do with a dollar and eighty-seven cents?"

At 7 o'clock the coffee was made and the frying-pan was on the back of the stove hot and ready to cook the chops.

Jim was never late. Della doubled the fob chain in her hand and sat on the corner of the table near the door that he always entered. Then she heard his step on the stair away down on the first flight, and she turned white for just a moment. She had a habit of saying a little silent prayer about the simplest everyday things, and now she whispered: "Please God, make him think I am still pretty."

The door opened and Jim stepped in and closed it. He

looked thin and very serious. Poor fellow, he was only twenty-two—and to be burdened with a family! He needed a new overcoat and he was without gloves.

Jim stopped inside the door, as immovable as a setter at the scent of quail. His eyes were fixed upon Della, and there was an expression in them that she could not read, and it terrified her. It was not anger, nor surprise, nor disapproval, nor horror, nor any of the sentiments that she had been prepared for. He simply stared at her fixedly with that peculiar expression on his face.

Della wriggled off the table and went for him.

"Jim, darling," she cried, "don't look at me that way. I had my hair cut off and sold because I couldn't have lived through Christmas without giving you a present. It'll grow out again—you won't mind, will you? I just had to do it. My hair grows awfully fast. Say 'Merry Christmas!' Jim, and let's be happy. You don't know what a nice—what a beautiful, nice gift I've got for you."

"You've cut off your hair?" asked Jim, laboriously, as if he had not arrived at that patent fact yet even after the hardest mental labor.

"Cut it off and sold it," said Della. "Don't you like me just as well, anyhow? I'm me without my hair, ain't I?"

Jim looked about the room curiously.

"You say your hair is gone?" he said, with an air almost of idiocy.

"You needn't look for it," said Della. "It's sold, I tell you—sold and gone, too. It's Christmas Eve, boy. Be good to me, for it went for you. Maybe the hairs of my head were numbered," she went on with sudden serious sweetness, "but nobody could ever count my love for you. Shall I put the chops on, Jim?"

Out of his trance Jim seemed quickly to wake. He enfolded his Della. For ten seconds let us regard with discreet scrutiny some inconsequential object in the other direction. Eight dollars a week or a million a year—what is the difference? A mathematician or a wit would give you the wrong answer. The magi brought valuable gifts, but that was not among them. This dark assertion will be illuminated later on.

Jim drew a package from his overcoat pocket and threw it upon the table.

"Don't make any mistake, Dell," he said, "about me. I don't think there's anything in the way of a haircut or a shave or a shampoo that could make me like my girl any less. But if you'll unwrap that package you may see why you had me going a while at first."

White fingers and nimble tore at the string and paper. And then an ecstatic scream of joy; and then, alas! a quick feminine change to hysterical tears and wails, necessitating the immediate employment of all the comforting powers of the lord of the flat.

For there lay The Combs—the set of combs, side and back, that Della had worshipped long in a Broadway window. Beautiful combs, pure tortoise shell, with jewelled rims—just the shade to wear in the beautiful vanished hair. They were expensive combs, she knew, and her heart had simply craved and yearned over them without the least hope of possession. And now, they were hers, but the tresses that should have adorned the coveted adornments were gone.

But she hugged them to her bosom, and at length she was able to look up with dim eyes and a smile and say: "My hair grows so fast, Jim!"

And then Della leaped up like a little singed cat and cried, "Oh, oh!"

Jim had not yet seen his beautiful present. She held it out to him eagerly upon her open palm. The dull precious metal seemed to flash with a reflection of her bright and ardent spirit.

"Isn't it a dandy, Jim? I hunted all over town to find it. You'll have to look at the time a hundred times a day now. Give me your watch. I want to see how it looks on it."

Instead of obeying, Jim tumbled down on the couch and put his hands under the back of his head and smiled.

"Dell," said he, "let's put our Christmas presents away and keep 'em a while. They're too nice to use just at present. I sold the watch to get the money to buy your combs. And now suppose you put the chops on."

The magi, as you know, were wise men—wonderfully wise men—who brought gifts to the Babe in the manger. They invented the art of giving Christmas presents. Being wise, their gifts were no doubt wise ones, possibly bearing the privilege of exchange in case of duplication. And here I have lamely related to you the uneventful chronicle of two foolish children in a flat who most unwisely sacrificed for each other the greatest treasures of their house. But in a last word to the wise of these days let it be said that of all who give gifts these two were the wisest. Of all who give and receive gifts, such as they are wisest. Everywhere they are wisest. They are the magi.

Tobin's Palm

TOBIN and me, the two of us, went down to Coney one day, for there was four dollars between us, and Tobin had need of distractions. For there was Katie Mahorner, his sweetheart, of County Sligo, lost since she started for America three months before with two hundred dollars, her own savings, and one hundred dollars from the sale of Tobin's inherited estate, a fine cottage and pig on the Bog Shannaugh. And since the letter that Tobin got saying that she had started to come to him not a bit of news had he heard or seen of Katie Mahorner. Tobin advertised in the papers, but nothing could be found of the colleen.

So, to Coney me and Tobin went, thinking that a turn at the chutes and the smell of the popcorn might raise the heart in his bosom. But Tobin was a hardheaded man, and the sadness stuck in his skin. He ground his teeth at the crying balloons; he cursed the moving pictures; and, though he would drink whenever asked, he scorned Punch and Judy, and was for licking the tintype men as they came.

So I gets him down a side way on a board walk where the attractions were some less violent. At a little six by eight stall Tobin halts, with a more human look in his eye.

"'Tis here," says he, "I will be diverted. I'll have the palm of me hand investigated by the wonderful palmist of the Nile, and see if what is to be will be."

Tobin was a believer in signs and the unnatural in nature. He possessed illegal convictions in his mind along the subjects of black cats, lucky numbers, and the weather predictions in the papers.

We went into the enchanted chicken coop, which was fixed mysterious with red cloth and pictures of hands with lines crossing 'em like a railroad centre. The sign over the door says it is Madame Zozo the Egyptian Palmist. There was a fat woman inside in a red jumper with pothooks and beasties embroidered upon it. Tobin gives her ten cents and extends one of his hands. She lifts Tobin's hand, which is own brother to the hoof of a drayhorse, and examines it to see whether 'tis a stone in the frog or a cast shoe he has come for.

"Man," says this Madame Zozo, "the line of your fate shows—"

"'Tis not me foot at all," says Tobin, interrupting. "Sure, 'tis no beauty, but ye hold the palm of me hand."

"The line shows," says the Madame, "that ye've not arrived at your time of life without bad luck. And there's more to come. The mount of Venus—or is that a stone bruise?—shows that ye've been in love. There's been trouble in your life on account of your sweetheart."

"'Tis Katie Mahorner she has references with," whispers Tobin to me in a loud voice to one side.

"I see," says the palmist, "a great deal of sorrow and tribulation with one whom ye cannot forget. I see the lines of designation point to the letter K and the letter M in her name."

"Whist!" says Tobin to me, "do ye hear that?"

"Look out," goes on the palmist, "for a dark man and a light woman; for they'll both bring ye trouble. Ye'll make a voyage upon the water very soon, and have a financial loss. I see one line that brings good luck. There's a man coming into your life who will fetch ye good fortune. Ye'll know him when ye see him by his crooked nose."

"Is his name set down?" asks Tobin. "'Twill be convenient in the way of greeting when he backs up to dump off the good luck."

"His name," says the palmist, thoughtful looking, "is not spelled out by the lines, but they indicate 'tis a long one, and the letter 'o' should be in it. There's no more to tell. Good-evening. Don't block up the door."

"'Tis wonderful how she knows," says Tobin as we walk to the pier.

As we squeezed through the gates a nigger man sticks his lighted segar against Tobin's ear, and there is trouble. Tobin hammers his neck, and the women squeal, and by presence of mind I drag the little man out of the way before the police comes. Tobin is always in an ugly mood when enjoying himself.

On the boat going back, when the man calls "Who wants the good-looking waiter?" Tobin tried to plead guilty, feeling the desire to blow the foam off a crock of suds, but when he felt in his pocket he found himself discharged for lack of evidence. Somebody had disturbed his change during the commotion. So we sat, dry, upon the stools, listening to the Dagoes fiddling on deck. If anything, Tobin was lower in spirits and less congenial with his misfortunes than when we started.

On a seat against the railing was a young woman dressed suitable for red automobiles, with hair the colour of an unsmoked meerschaum. In passing by, Tobin kicks her foot without intentions, and, being polite to ladies when in drink, he tries to give his hat a twist while apologising. But he knocks it off, and the wind carries it overboard.

Tobin came back and sat down, and I began to look out for him, for the man's adversities were becoming frequent. He was apt, when pushed so close by hard luck, to kick the best dressed man he could see, and try to take command of the boat.

Presently Tobin grabs my arm and says, excited: "Jawn," says he, "do ye know what we're doing? We're taking a voyage upon the water."

"There now," says I; "subdue yeself. The boat'll land in ten minutes more."

"Look," says he, "at the light lady upon the bench. And have ye forgotten the nigger man that burned me ear? And isn't the money I had gone—a dollar sixty-five it was?"

I thought he was no more than summing up his catastrophes so as to get violent with good excuse, as men will do, and I tried to make him understand such things was trifles.

"Listen," says Tobin. "Ye've no ear for the gift of prophecy or the miracles of the inspired. What did the palmist lady tell ye out of me hand? 'Tis coming true before your eyes. 'Look out,' says she, 'for a dark man and a light woman; they'll bring ye trouble.' Have ye forgot the nigger man, though he got some of it back from me fist? Can ye show me a lighter woman than the blonde lady that was the cause of me hat falling in the water? And where's the dollar sixty-five I had in me vest when we left the shooting gallery?"

The way Tobin put it, it did seem to corroborate the art of prediction, though it looked to me that these accidents could happen to any one at Coney without the implication of palmistry.

Tobin got up and walked around on deck, looking close at the passengers out of his little red eyes. I asked him the interpretation of his movements. Ye never know what Tobin has in his mind until he begins to carry it out.

"Ye should know," says he, "I'm working out the salvation promised by the lines in me palm. I'm looking for the crooked-nose man that's to bring the good luck. 'Tis all that will save us. Jawn, did ye ever see a straighter-nosed gang of hellions in the days of your life?"

'Twas the nine-thirty boat, and we landed and walked uptown through Twenty-second Street, Tobin being without his hat.

On a street corner, standing under a gas-light and looking over the elevated road at the moon, was a man. A long man he was, dressed decent, with a segar between his teeth, and I saw that his nose made two twists from bridge to end, like the wriggle of a snake. Tobin saw it at the same time, and I heard him breathe hard like a horse when you take the saddle off. He went straight up to the man, and I went with him.

"Good-night to ye," Tobin says to the man. The man takes out his segar and passes the compliments, sociable.

"Would ye hand us your name," asks Tobin, "and let us look at the size of it? It may be our duty to become acquainted with ye."

"My name" says the man, polite, "is Friedenhausman—Maximus G. Friedenhausman."

"'Tis the right length," says Tobin. "Do you spell it with an 'o' anywhere down the stretch of it?"

"I do not," says the man.

"*Can* ye spell it with an 'o'?" inquires Tobin, turning anxious.

"If your conscience," says the man with the nose, "is indisposed toward foreign idioms ye might, to please yourself, smuggle the letter into the penultimate syllable."

"'Tis well," says Tobin. "Ye're in the presence of Jawn Malone and Daniel Tobin."

"'Tis highly appreciated," says the man, with a bow. "And now since I cannot conceive that ye would hold a spelling bee upon the street corner, will ye name some reasonable excuse for being at large?"

"By the two signs," answers Tobin, trying to explain, "which ye display according to the reading of the Egyptian palmist from the sole of me hand, ye've been nominated to offset with good luck the lines of trouble leading to the nigger man and the blonde lady with her feet crossed in the boat, besides the financial loss of a dollar sixty-five, all so far fulfilled according to Hoyle."

The man stopped smoking and looked at me.

"Have ye any amendments," he asks, "to offer to that statement, or are ye one too? I thought by the looks of ye ye might have him in charge."

"None," says I to him, "except that as one horseshoe resembles another so are ye the picture of good luck as predicted by the hand of me friend. If not, then the lines of Danny's hand may have been crossed, I don't know."

"There's two of ye," says the man with the nose, looking up and down for the sight of a policeman. "I've enjoyed your company immense. Good-night."

With that he shoves his segar in his mouth and moves across the street, stepping fast. But Tobin sticks close to one side of him and me at the other.

"What!" says he, stopping on the opposite sidewalk and pushing back his hat; "do ye follow me? I tell ye," he says, very loud, "I'm proud to have met ye. But it is my desire to be rid of ye. I am off to me home."

"Do," says Tobin, leaning against his sleeve. "Do be off to your home. And I will sit at the door of it till ye come out in the morning. For the dependence is upon ye to obviate the curse of the nigger man and the blonde lady and the financial loss of the one-sixty-five."

"'Tis a strange hallucination," says the man, turning to me as a more reasonable lunatic. "Hadn't ye better get him home?"

"Listen, man," says I to him. "Daniel Tobin is as sensible as he ever was. Maybe he is a bit deranged on account of having drink enough to disturb but not enough to settle his wits, but he is no more than following out the legitimate path of his superstitions and predicaments, which I will explain to you." With that I relates the facts about the palmist lady and how the finger of suspicion points to him as an instrument of good fortune. "Now, understand," I concludes, "my position in this riot. I am the friend of me friend Tobin, according to me interpretations. 'Tis easy to be a friend to the prosperous, for it pays; 'tis not hard to be a friend to the poor, for ye get puffed up by gratitude and have your picture printed standing in front of a tenement with a scuttle of coal and an orphan in each hand. But it strains the art of friendship to be true friend to a born fool. And that's what I'm doing," says I, "for, in my opinion, there's no fortune to be read from the palm of me hand that wasn't printed there with the handle of a pick. And, though ye've got the crookedest nose in New York City, I misdoubt that all the fortune-tellers doing business could milk good luck from ye. But the lines of Danny's hand pointed to ye fair, and I'll assist him to experiment with ye until he's convinced ye're dry."

After that the man turns, sudden, to laughing. He leans against a corner and laughs considerable. Then he claps me and Tobin on the backs of us and takes us by an arm apiece.

"'Tis my mistake," says he. "How could I be expecting anything so fine and wonderful to be turning the corner upon me? I came near being found unworthy. Hard by," says he, "is a café, snug and suitable for the entertainment of idiosyncrasies. Let us go there and have drink while we discuss the unavailability of the categorical."

So saying, he marched me and Tobin to the back room of a saloon, and ordered the drinks, and laid the money on the table. He looks at me and Tobin like brothers of his, and we have the segars.

"Ye must know," says the man of destiny, "that me walk in life is one that is called the literary. I wander abroad be night seeking idiosyncrasies in the masses and truth in the heavens above. When ye came upon me I was in contemplation of the elevated road in conjunction with the chief luminary of night. The rapid transit is poetry and art: the moon but a tedious, dry body, moving by rote. But these are private opinions, for, in the business of literature, the conditions are reversed. 'Tis me hope to be writing a book to explain the strange things I have discovered in life."

"Ye will put me in a book," says Tobin, disgusted; "will ye put me in a book?"

"I will not," says the man, "for the covers will not hold ye. Not yet. The best I can do is to enjoy ye meself, for the time is not ripe for destroying the limitations of print. Ye would look fantastic in type. All alone by meself must I drink this cup of joy. But, I thank ye, boys; I am truly grateful."

"The talk of ye," says Tobin, blowing through his moustache and pounding the table with his fist, "is an eyesore to me patience. There was good luck promised out of the crook of your nose, but ye bear fruit like the bang of a drum. Ye resemble, with your noise of books, the wind blowing through a crack. Sure, now, I would be thinking the palm of me hand lied but for the coming true of the nigger man and the blonde lady and—"

"Whist!" says the long man; "would ye be led astray by physiognomy? Me nose will do what it can within bounds. Let us have these glasses filled again, for 'tis good to keep idiosyncrasies well moistened, they being subject to deterioration in a dry moral atmosphere."

So, the man of literature makes good, to my notion, for he pays, cheerful, for everything, the capital of me and Tobin being exhausted by prediction. But Tobin is sore, and drinks quiet, with the red showing in his eye.

By and by we moved out, for 'twas eleven o'clock, and stands a bit upon the sidewalk. And then the man says he must be going home, and invites me and Tobin to walk that way. We arrives on a side street two blocks away where there is a stretch of brick houses with high stoops and iron fences. The man stops at one of them and looks up at the top windows which he finds dark.

"'Tis me humble dwelling," says he, "and I begin to perceive by the signs that me wife has retired to slumber. Therefore I will venture a bit in the way of hospitality. 'Tis me wish that ye enter the basement room, where we dine, and partake of a reasonable refreshment. There will be some fine cold fowl and cheese and a bottle or two of ale. Ye will be welcome to enter and eat, for I am indebted to ye for diversions."

The appetite and conscience of me and Tobin was congenial to the proposition, though 'twas sticking hard in Danny's superstitions to think that a few drinks and a cold lunch should represent the good fortune promised by the palm of his hand.

"Step down the steps," says the man with the crooked nose, "and I will enter by the door above and let ye in. I will ask the new girl we have in the kitchen," says he, "to make ye a pot of coffee to drink before ye go. 'Tis fine coffee Katie Mahorner makes for a green girl just landed three months. Step in," says the man, "and I'll send her down to ye."

A Cosmopolite in a Café

AT midnight the café was crowded. By some chance the little table at which I sat had escaped the eye of incomers, and two vacant chairs at it extended their arms with venal hospitality to the influx of patrons.

And then a cosmopolite sat in one of them, and I was glad, for I held a theory that since Adam no true citizen of the world has existed. We hear of them, and we see foreign labels on much luggage, but we find travellers instead of cosmopolites.

I invoke your consideration of the scene—the marble-topped tables, the range of leather-upholstered wall seats, the gay company, the ladies dressed in demi-state toilets, speaking in an exquisite visible chorus of taste, economy, opulence or art; the sedulous and largess-loving *garçons*, the music wisely catering to all with its raids upon the composers; the *mélange* of talk and laughter—and, if you will, the Würzburger in the tall glass cones that bend to your lips as a ripe cherry sways on its branch to the beak of a robber jay. I was told by a sculptor from Mauch Chunk that the scene was truly Parisian.

My cosmopolite was named E. Rushmore Coglan, and he will be heard from next summer at Coney Island. He is to establish a new "attraction" there, he informed me, offering kingly diversion. And then his conversation rang along parallels of latitude and longitude. He took the great, round world in his hand, so to speak, familiarly, contemptuously, and it seemed no larger than the seed of a Maraschino cherry in a *table d'hôte* grape fruit. He spoke disrespectfully of the equator, he skipped from continent to continent, he derided the zones, he mopped up the high seas with his napkin. With a wave of his hand he would speak of a certain bazaar in Hyderabad.

Whiff! He would have you on skis in Lapland. Zip! Now you rode the breakers with the Kanakas at Kealaikahiki. Presto! He dragged you through an Arkansas post-oak swamp, let you dry for a moment on the alkali plains of his Idaho ranch, then whirled you into the society of Viennese archdukes. Anon he would be telling you of a cold he acquired in a Chicago lake breeze and how old Escamila cured it in Buenos Ayres with a hot infusion of the *chuchula* weed. You would have addressed a letter to "E. Rushmore Coglan, Esq., the Earth, Solar System, the Universe," and have mailed it, feeling confident that it would be delivered to him.

I was sure that I had found at last the one true cosmopolite since Adam, and I listened to his worldwide discourse fearful lest I should discover in it the local note of the mere globe-trotter. But his opinions never fluttered or drooped; he was as impartial to cities, countries and continents as the winds or gravitation.

And as E. Rushmore Coglan prattled of this little planet I thought with glee of a great almost-cosmopolite who wrote for the whole world and dedicated himself to Bombay. In a poem he has to say that there is pride and rivalry between the cities of the earth, and that "the men that breed from them, they traffic up and down, but cling to their cities' hem as a child to the mother's gown." And whenever they walk "by roaring streets unknown" they remember their native city "most faithful, foolish, fond; making her mere-breathed name their bond upon their bond." And my glee was roused because I had caught Mr. Kipling napping. Here I had found a man not made from dust; one who had no narrow boasts of birthplace or country, one who, if he bragged at all, would brag of his whole round globe against the Martians and the inhabitants of the Moon.

Expression on these subjects was precipitated from E.

Rushmore Coglan by the third corner to our table. While Coglan was describing to me the topography along the Siberian Railway the orchestra glided into a medley. The concluding air was "Dixie," and as the exhilarating notes tumbled forth they were almost overpowered by a great clapping of hands from almost every table.

It is worth a paragraph to say that this remarkable scene can be witnessed every evening in numerous cafés in the City of New York. Tons of brew have been consumed over theories to account for it. Some have conjectured hastily that all Southerners in town hie themselves to cafés at nightfall. This applause of the "rebel" air in a Northern city does puzzle a little; but it is not insolvable. The war with Spain, many years' generous mint and watermelon crops, a few long-shot winners at the New Orleans race-track, and the brilliant banquets given by the Indiana and Kansas citizens who compose the North Carolina Society have made the South rather a "fad" in Manhattan. Your manicure will lisp softly that your left forefinger reminds her so much of a gentleman's in Richmond, Va. Oh, certainly; but many a lady has to work now—the war, you know.

When "Dixie" was being played a dark-haired young man sprang up from somewhere with a Mosby guerrilla yell and waved frantically his soft-brimmed hat. Then he strayed through the smoke, dropped into the vacant chair at our table and pulled out cigarettes.

The evening was at the period when reserve is thawed. One of us mentioned three Würzburgers to the waiter; the dark-haired young man acknowledged his inclusion in the order by a smile and a nod. I hastened to ask him a question because I wanted to try out a theory I had.

"Would you mind telling me," I began, "whether you are from—"

The fist of E. Rushmore Coglan banged the table and I was jarred into silence.

"Excuse me," said he, "but that's a question I never like to hear asked. What does it matter where a man is from? Is it fair to judge a man by his post-office address? Why, I've seen Kentuckians who hated whiskey, Virginians who weren't descended from Pocahontas, Indianians who hadn't written a novel, Mexicans who didn't wear velvet trousers with silver dollars sewed along the seams, funny Englishmen, spendthrift Yankees, cold-blooded Southerners, narrow-minded Westerners, and New Yorkers who were too busy to stop for an hour on the street to watch a one-armed grocer's clerk do up cranberries in paper bags. Let a man be a man and don't handicap him with the label of any section."

"Pardon me," I said, "but my curiosity was not altogether an idle one. I know the South, and when the band plays 'Dixie' I like to observe. I have formed the belief that the man who applauds that air with special violence and ostensible sectional loyalty is invariably a native of either Secaucus, N.J., or the district between Murray Hill Lyceum and the Harlem River, this city. I was about to put my opinion to the test by inquiring of this gentleman when you interrupted with your own—larger theory, I must confess."

And now the dark-haired young man spoke to me, and it became evident that his mind also moved along its own set of grooves.

"I should like to be a periwinkle," said he, mysteriously, "on the top of a valley, and sing tooralloo-ralloo."

This was clearly too obscure, so I turned again to Coglan.

"I've been around the world twelve times," said he. "I know an Esquimau in Upernavik who sends to Cincinnati for his neckties, and I saw a goat-herder in Uruguay who won a prize in a Battle Creek breakfast food puzzle competition. I pay rent on a room in Cairo, Egypt, and another in Yokohama all the year around. I've got slippers waiting for me in a tea-house in Shanghai, and I don't have to tell 'em how to cook my eggs in Rio de Janeiro or Seattle. It's a mighty little old world. What's the use of bragging about being from the North, or the South, or the old manor house in the dale, or Euclid avenue, Cleveland, or Pike's Peak, or Fairfax County, Va., or Hooligan's Flats or any place? It'll be a better world when we quit being fools about some mildewed town or ten acres of swampland just because we happened to be born there."

"You seem to be a genuine cosmopolite," I said admiringly. "But it also seems that you would decry patriotism."

"A relic of the stone age," declared Coglan, warmly. "We are all brothers—Chinamen, Englishmen, Zulus, Patagonians and the people in the bend of the Kaw River. Some day all this petty pride in one's city or State or section or country will be wiped out, and we'll all be citizens of the world, as we ought to be."

"But while you are wandering in foreign lands," I persisted, "do not your thoughts revert to some spot—some dear and—"

"Nary a spot," interrupted E. R. Coglan, flippantly. "The terrestrial, globular, planetary hunk of matter, slightly flattened at the poles, and known as the Earth, is my abode. I've met a good many object-bound citizens of this country abroad. I've seen men from Chicago sit in a gondola in Venice on a moonlight night and brag about their drainage canal. I've seen a Southerner on being introduced to the King of England hand that monarch, without batting his eyes, the information that his grand-aunt on his mother's side was related by marriage to the Perkinses, of Charleston. I knew a New Yorker who was kidnapped for ransom by some Afghanistan bandits. His people sent over the money and he came back to Kabul with the agent. 'Afghanistan?' the natives said to him through an interpreter. 'Well, not so slow, do you think?' 'Oh, I don't know,' says he, and he begins to tell them about a cab driver at Sixth avenue and Broadway. Those ideas don't suit me. I'm not tied down to anything that isn't 8,000 miles in diameter. Just put me down as E. Rushmore Coglan, citizen of the terrestrial sphere."

My cosmopolite made a large adieu and left me, for he thought he saw some one through the chatter and smoke whom he knew. So I was left with the would-be periwinkle, who was reduced to Würzburger without further ability to voice his aspirations to perch, melodious, upon the summit of a valley.

I sat reflecting upon my evident cosmopolite and wondering how the poet had managed to miss him. He was my discovery and I believed in him. How was it? "The men that breed from them they traffic up and down, but cling to their cities' hem as a child to the mother's gown."

Not so E. Rushmore Coglan. With the whole world for his—

My meditations were interrupted by a tremendous noise and conflict in another part of the café. I saw above the heads of the seated patrons E. Rushmore Coglan and a stranger to me engaged in terrific battle. They fought between the tables like Titans, and glasses crashed, and men caught their hats up and were knocked down, and a brunette screamed, and a blonde began to sing "Teasing."

My cosmopolite was sustaining the pride and reputation of the Earth when the waiters closed in on both combatants with their famous flying wedge formation and bore them outside, still resisting.

I called McCarthy, one of the French *garçons*, and asked him the cause of the conflict.

"The man with the red tie" (that was my cosmopolite), said

he, "got hot on account of things said about the bum sidewalks and water supply of the place he come from by the other guy."

"Why," said I, bewildered, "that man is a citizen of the world—a cosmopolite. He—"

"Originally from Mattawamkeag, Maine, he said," continued McCarthy, "and he wouldn't stand for no knockin' the place."

Between Rounds

THE May moon shone bright upon the private boarding-house of Mrs. Murphy. By reference to the almanac a large amount of territory will be discovered upon which its rays also fell. Spring was in its heydey, with hay fever soon to follow. The parks were green with new leaves and buyers for the Western and Southern trade. Flowers and summer-resort agents were blowing; the air and answers to Lawson were growing milder; hand-organs, fountains and pinochle were playing everywhere.

The windows of Mrs. Murphy's boarding-house were open. A group of boarders were seated on the high stoop upon round, flat mats like German pancakes.

In one of the second-floor front windows Mrs. McCaskey awaited her husband. Supper was cooling on the table. Its heat went into Mrs. McCaskey.

At nine Mr. McCaskey came. He carried his coat on his arm and his pipe in his teeth; and he apologised for disturbing the boarders on the steps as he selected spots of stone between them on which to set his size 9, width Ds.

As he opened the door of his room he received a surprise. Instead of the usual stove-lid or potato-masher for him to dodge, came only words.

Mr. McCaskey reckoned that the benign May moon had softened the breast of his spouse.

"I heard ye," came the oral substitutes for kitchenware. "Ye can apollygise to riff-raff of the streets for settin' yer unhandy feet on the tails of their frocks, but ye'd walk on the neck of yer wife the length of a clothes-line without so much as a 'Kiss me fut,' and I'm sure it's that long from rubberin' out the windy for ye and the victuals cold such as there's money to buy after drinkin' up yer wages at Gallegher's every Saturday evenin', and the gas man here twice to-day for his."

"Woman!" said Mr. McCaskey, dashing his coat and hat upon a chair, "the noise of ye is an insult to me appetite. When ye run down politeness ye take the mortar from between the bricks of the foundations of society. 'Tis no more than exercisin' the acrimony of a gentleman when ye ask the dissent of ladies blockin' the way for steppin' between them. Will ye bring the pig's face of ye out of the windy and see to the food?"

Mrs. McCaskey arose heavily and went to the stove. There was something in her manner that warned Mr. McCaskey. When the corners of her mouth went down suddenly like a barometer it usually foretold a fall of crockery and tinware.

"Pig's face, is it?" said Mrs. McCaskey, and hurled a stewpan full of bacon and turnips at her lord.

Mr. McCaskey was no novice at repartee. He knew what should follow the entrée. On the table was a roast sirloin of pork, garnished with shamrocks. He retorted with this, and drew the appropriate return of a bread pudding in an earthen dish. A hunk of Swiss cheese accurately thrown by her husband struck Mrs. McCaskey below one eye. When she replied with a well-aimed coffee-pot full of a hot, black, semi-fragrant liquid the battle, according to courses, should have ended.

But Mr. McCaskey was no 50-cent *table d'hôter*. Let cheap Bohemians consider coffee the end, if they would. Let them make that *faux pas*. He was foxier still. Finger-bowls were not beyond the compass of his experience. They were not to be had in the Pension Murphy; but their equivalent was at hand. Triumphantly he sent the granite-ware wash basin at the head of his matrimonial adversary. Mrs. McCaskey dodged in time. She reached for a flatiron, with which, as a sort of cordial, she hoped to bring the gastronomical duel to a close. But a loud, wailing scream downstairs caused both her and Mr. McCaskey to pause in a sort of involuntary armistice.

On the sidewalk at the corner of the house Policeman Cleary was standing with one ear upturned, listening to the crash of household utensils.

"'Tis Jawn McCaskey and his missis at it again," meditated the policeman. "I wonder shall I go up and stop the row. I will not. Married folks they are; and few pleasures they have. 'Twill not last long. Sure, they'll have to borrow more dishes to keep it up with."

And just then came the loud scream below-stairs, betokening fear or dire extremity. "'Tis probably the cat," said Policeman Cleary, and walked hastily in the other direction.

The boarders on the steps were fluttered. Mr. Toomey, an insurance solicitor by birth and an investigator by profession, went inside to analyse the scream. He returned with the news that Mrs. Murphy's little boy, Mike, was lost. Following the messenger, out bounced Mrs. Murphy—two hundred pounds in tears and hysterics, clutching the air and howling to the sky for the loss of thirty pounds of freckles and mischief. Bathos, truly; but Mr. Toomey sat down at the side of Miss Purdy, millinery, and their hands came together in sympathy. The two old maids, Misses Walsh, who complained every day about the noise in the halls, inquired immediately if anybody had looked behind the clock.

Major Grigg, who sat by his fat wife on the top step, arose and buttoned his coat. "The little one lost?" he exclaimed. "I will scour the city." His wife never allowed him out after dark. But now she said: "Go, Ludovic!" in a baritone voice. "Whoever can look upon that mother's grief without springing to her relief has a heart of stone." "Give me some thirty or—sixty cents, my love," said the Major. "Lost children sometimes stray far. I may need carfares."

Old man Denny, hall room, fourth floor back, who sat on the lowest step, trying to read a paper by the street lamp, turned over a page to follow up the article about the carpenters' strike. Mrs. Murphy shrieked to the moon: "Oh, ar-r-Mike, f'r Gawd's sake, where is me little bit av a boy?"

"When'd ye see him last?" asked old man Denny, with one eye on the report of the Building Trades League.

"Oh," wailed Mrs. Murphy, "'twas yisterday, or maybe four hours ago! I dunno. But it's lost he is, me little boy Mike. He was playin' on the sidewalk only this mornin'—or was it Wednesday? I'm that busy with work, 'tis hard to keep up with dates. But I've looked the house over from top to cellar, and it's gone he is. Oh, for the love av Hiven—"

Silent, grim, colossal, the big city has ever stood against its revilers. They call it hard as iron; they say that no pulse of pity beats in its bosom; they compare its streets with lonely forests and deserts of lava. But beneath the hard crust of the lobster is found a delectable and luscious food. Perhaps a different simile would have been wiser. Still, nobody should take offence. We would call no one a lobster without good and sufficient claws.

No calamity so touches the common heart of humanity as does the straying of a little child. Their feet are so uncertain and feeble; the ways are so steep and strange.

Major Griggs hurried down to the corner, and up the avenue into Billy's place. "Gimme a rye-high," he said to the servitor. "Haven't seen a bow-legged, dirty-faced little devil of a six-year-old lost kid around here anywhere, have you?"

Mr. Toomey retained Miss Purdy's hand on the steps. "Think of that dear little babe," said Miss Purdy, "lost from his mother's side—perhaps already fallen beneath the iron hoofs of galloping steeds—oh, isn't it dreadful?"

"Ain't that right?" agreed Mr. Toomey, squeezing her hand. "Say I start out and help look for um!"

"Perhaps," said Miss Purdy, "you should. But, oh, Mr. Toomey, you are so dashing—so reckless—suppose in your enthusiasm some accident should befall you, then what—"

Old man Denny read on about the arbitration agreement, with one finger on the lines.

In the second floor front Mr. and Mrs. McCaskey came to the window to recover their second wind. Mr. McCaskey was scooping turnips out of his vest with a crooked forefinger, and his lady was wiping an eye that the salt of the roast pork had not benefited. They heard the outcry below, and thrust their heads out of the window.

"'Tis little Mike is lost," said Mrs. McCaskey, in a hushed voice, "the beautiful, little, trouble-making angel of a gossoon!"

"The bit of a boy mislaid?" said Mr. McCaskey, leaning out of the window. "Why, now, that's bad enough, entirely. The childer, they be different. If 'twas a woman I'd be willin', for they leave peace behind 'em when they go."

Disregarding the thrust, Mrs. McCaskey caught her husband's arm.

"Jawn," she said, sentimentally, "Missis Murphy's little bye is lost. 'Tis a great city for losing little boys. Six years old he was. Jawn, 'tis the same age our little bye would have been if we had had one six years ago."

"We never did," said Mr. McCaskey, lingering with the fact.

"But if we had, Jawn, think what sorrow would be in our hearts this night, with our little Phelan run away and stolen in the city nowheres at all."

"Ye talk foolishness," said Mr. McCaskey. "'Tis Pat he would be named, after me old father in Cantrim."

"Ye lie!" said Mrs. McCaskey, without anger. "Me brother

was worth tin dozen bog-trotting McCaskeys. After him would the bye be named." She leaned over the window-sill and looked down at the hurrying and bustle below.

"Jawn," said Mrs. McCaskey, softly, "I'm sorry I was hasty wid ye."

"'Twas hasty puddin', as ye say," said her husband, "and hurry-up turnips and get-a-move-on-ye coffee. 'Twas what ye could call a quick lunch, all right, and tell no lie."

Mrs. McCaskey slipped her arm inside her husband's and took his rough hand in hers.

"Listen at the cryin' of poor Mrs. Murphy," she said. "'Tis an awful thing for a bit of a bye to be lost in this great big city. If 'twas our little Phelan, Jawn, I'd be breakin' me heart."

Awkwardly Mr. McCaskey withdrew his hand. But he laid it around the nearing shoulder of his wife.

"'Tis foolishness, of course," said he, roughly, "but I'd be cut up some meself if our little Pat was kidnapped or anything. But there never was any childer for us. Sometimes I've been ugly and hard with ye, Judy. Forget it."

They leaned together, and looked down at the heart-drama being acted below.

Long they sat thus. People surged along the sidewalk, crowding, questioning, filling the air with rumours, and inconsequent surmises. Mrs. Murphy ploughed back and forth in their midst, like a soft mountain down which plunged an audible cataract of tears. Couriers came and went.

Loud voices and a renewed uproar were raised in front of the boarding-house.

"What's up now, Judy?" asked Mr. McCaskey.

"'Tis Missis Murphy's voice," said Mrs. McCaskey, harking. "She says she's after finding little Mike asleep behind the roll of old linoleum under the bed in her room."

Mr. McCaskey laughed loudly.

"That's yer Phelan," he shouted, sardonically. "Divil a bit would a Pat have done that trick. If the bye we never had is strayed and stole, by the powers, call him Phelan, and see him hide out under the bed like a mangy pup."

Mrs. McCaskey arose heavily, and went toward the dish closet, with the corners of her mouth drawn down.

Policeman Cleary came back around the corner as the crowd dispersed. Surprised, he upturned an ear toward the McCaskey apartment, where the crash of irons and chinaware and the ring of hurled kitchen utensils seemed as loud as before. Policeman Cleary took out his timepiece.

"By the deported snakes!" he exclaimed, "Jawn McCaskey and his lady have been fightin' for an hour and a quarter by the watch. The missis could give him forty pounds weight. Strength to his arm."

Policeman Cleary strolled back around the corner.

Old man Denny folded his paper and hurried up the steps just as Mrs. Murphy was about to lock the door for the night.

The Skylight Room

FIRST Mrs. Parker would show you the double parlours. You would not dare to interrupt her description of their advantages and of the merits of the gentleman who had occupied them for eight years. Then you would manage to stammer forth the confession that you were neither a doctor nor a dentist. Mrs. Parker's manner of receiving the admission was such that you could never afterward entertain the same feeling toward your parents, who had neglected to train you up in one of the professions that fitted Mrs. Parker's parlours.

Next you ascended one flight of stairs and looked at the second-floor-back at $8. Convinced by her second-floor manner that it was worth the $12 that Mr. Toosenberry always paid for it until he left to take charge of his brother's orange plantation in Florida near Palm Beach, where Mrs. McIntyre always spent the winters that had the double front room with private bath, you managed to babble that you wanted something still cheaper.

If you survived Mrs. Parker's scorn, you were taken to look at Mr. Skidder's large hall room on the third floor. Mr. Skidder's room was not vacant. He wrote plays and smoked cigarettes in it all day long. But every room-hunter was made to visit his room to admire the lambrequins. After each visit, Mr. Skidder, from the fright caused by possible eviction, would pay something on his rent.

Then—oh, then—if you still stood on one foot, with your hot hand clutching the three moist dollars in your pocket, and hoarsely proclaimed your hideous and culpable poverty, nevermore would Mrs. Parker be cicerone of yours. She would honk loudly the word "Clara," she would show you her back, and march downstairs. Then Clara, the coloured maid, would escort you up the carpeted ladder that served for the fourth flight, and show you the Skylight Room. It occupied 7×8 feet of floor space at the middle of the hall. On each side of it was a dark lumber closet or storeroom.

In it was an iron cot, a washstand and a chair. A shelf was the dresser. Its four bare walls seemed to close in upon you like the sides of a coffin. Your hand crept to your throat, you gasped, you looked up as from a well—and breathed once more. Through the glass of the little skylight you saw a square of blue infinity.

"Two dollars, suh," Clara would say in her half-contemptuous, half-Tuskegeenial tones.

One day Miss Leeson came hunting for a room. She carried a typewriter made to be lugged around by a much larger lady. She was a very little girl, with eyes and hair that had kept on growing after she had stopped and that always looked as if they were saying: "Goodness me! Why didn't you keep up with us?"

Mrs. Parker showed her the double parlours. "In this closet," she said, "one could keep a skeleton or anaesthetic or coal—"

"But I am neither a doctor nor a dentist," said Miss Leeson, with a shiver.

Mrs. Parker gave her the incredulous, pitying, sneering, icy stare that she kept for those who failed to qualify as doctors or dentists, and led the way to the second floor back.

"Eight dollars?" said Miss Leeson. "Dear me! I'm not Hetty if I do look green. I'm just a poor little working girl. Show me something higher and lower."

Mr. Skidder jumped and strewed the floor with cigarette stubs at the rap on his door.

"Excuse me, Mr. Skidder," said Mrs. Parker, with her demon's smile at his pale looks. "I didn't know you were in. I asked the lady to have a look at your lambrequins."

"They're too lovely for anything," said Miss Leeson, smiling in exactly the way the angels do.

After they had gone Mr. Skidder got very busy erasing the tall, black-haired heroine from his latest (unproduced) play and inserting a small, roguish one with heavy, bright hair and vivacious features.

"Anna Held'll jump at it," said Mr. Skidder to himself, putting his feet up against the lambrequins and disappearing in a cloud of smoke like an aerial cuttlefish.

Presently the tocsin call of "Clara!" sounded to the world the state of Miss Leeson's purse. A dark goblin seized her, mounted a Stygian stairway, thrust her into a vault with a glimmer of light in its top and muttered the menacing and cabalistic words "Two dollars!"

"I'll take it!" sighed Miss Leeson, sinking down upon the squeaky iron bed.

Every day Miss Leeson went out to work. At night she brought home papers with handwriting on them and made copies with her typewriter. Sometimes she had no work at night, and then she would sit on the steps of the high stoop with the other roomers. Miss Leeson was not intended for a sky-light room when the plans were drawn for her creation. She was gay-hearted and full of tender, whimsical fancies. Once she let Mr. Skidder read to her three acts of his great (unpublished) comedy, "It's No Kid; or, The Heir of the Subway."

There was rejoicing among the gentlemen roomers whenever Miss Leeson had time to sit on the steps for an hour or two. But Miss Longnecker, the tall blonde who taught in a public school and said, "Well, really!" to everything you said, sat on the top step and sniffed. And Miss Dorn, who shot at the moving ducks at Coney every Sunday and worked in a department store, sat on the bottom step and sniffed. Miss Leeson sat on the middle step and the men would quickly group around her.

Especially Mr. Skidder, who had cast her in his mind for the star part in a private, romantic (unspoken) drama in real life. And especially Mr. Hoover, who was forty-five, fat, flush and foolish. And especially very young Mr. Evans, who set up a hollow cough to induce her to ask him to leave off cigarettes. The men voted her "the funniest and jolliest ever," but the sniffs on the top step and the lower step were implacable.

* * * * * * *

I pray you let the drama halt while Chorus stalks to the footlights and drops an epicedian tear upon the fatness of Mr. Hoover. Tune the pipes to the tragedy of tallow, the bane of bulk, the calamity of corpulence. Tried out, Falstaff might have rendered more romance to the ton than would have Romeo's rickety ribs to the ounce. A lover may sigh, but he must not puff. To the train of Momus are the fat men remanded. In vain beats the faithfullest heart above a 52-inch belt. Avaunt, Hoover! Hoover, forty-five, flush and foolish, might carry off Helen herself; Hoover, forty-five, flush, foolish and fat is meat for perdition. There was never a chance for you, Hoover.

As Mrs. Parker's roomers sat thus one summer's evening, Miss Leeson looked up into the firmament and cried with her little gay laugh:

"Why, there's Billy Jackson! I can see him from down here, too."

All looked up—some at the windows of skyscrapers, some casting about for an airship, Jackson-guided.

"It's that star," explained Miss Leeson, pointing with a tiny finger. "Not the big one that twinkles—the steady blue one near it. I can see it every night through my skylight. I named it Billy Jackson."

"Well, really!" said Miss Longnecker. "I didn't know you were an astronomer, Miss Leeson."

"Oh, yes," said the small star gazer, "I know as much as any of them about the style of sleeves they're going to wear next fall in Mars."

"Well, really!" said Miss Longnecker. "The star you refer to is Gamma, of the constellation Cassiopeia. It is nearly of the second magnitude, and its meridian passage is—"

"Oh," said the very young Mr. Evans, "I think Billy Jackson is a much better name for it."

"Same here," said Mr. Hoover, loudly breathing defiance to Miss Longnecker. "I think Miss Leeson has just as much right to name stars as any of those old astrologers had."

"Well, really!" said Miss Longnecker.

"I wonder whether it's a shooting star," remarked Miss Dorn. "I hit nine ducks and a rabbit out of ten in the gallery at Coney Sunday."

"He doesn't show up very well from down here," said Miss Leeson. "You ought to see him from my room. You know you can see stars even in the daytime from the bottom of a well. At night my room is like the shaft of a coal mine, and it makes Billy Jackson look like the big diamond pin that Night fastens her kimono with."

There came a time after that when Miss Leeson brought no formidable papers home to copy. And when she went out in the morning, instead of working, she went from office to office and let her heart melt away in the drip of cold refusals transmitted through insolent office boys. This went on.

There came an evening when she wearily climbed Mrs.

Parker's stoop at the hour when she always returned from her dinner at the restaurant. But she had had no dinner.

As she stepped into the hall Mr. Hoover met her and seized his chance. He asked her to marry him, and his fatness hovered above her like an avalanche. She dodged, and caught the balustrade. He tried for her hand, and she raised it and smote him weakly in the face. Step by step she went up, dragging herself by the railing. She passed Mr. Skidder's door as he was red-inking a stage direction for Myrtle Delorme (Miss Leeson) in his (unaccepted) comedy, to "pirouette across stage from L to the side of the Count." Up the carpeted ladder she crawled at last and opened the door of the skylight room.

She was too weak to light the lamp or to undress. She fell upon the iron cot, her fragile body scarcely hollowing the worn springs. And in that Erebus of the skylight room, she slowly raised her heavy eyelids, and smiled.

For Billy Jackson was shining down on her, calm and bright and constant through the skylight. There was no world about her. She was sunk in a pit of blackness, with but that small square of pallid light framing the star that she had so whimsically and oh, so ineffectually named. Miss Longnecker must be right; it was Gamma, of the constellation Cassiopeia, and not Billy Jackson. And yet she could not let it be Gamma.

As she lay on her back she tried twice to raise her arm. The third time she got two thin fingers to her lips and blew a kiss out of the black pit to Billy Jackson. Her arm fell back limply.

"Good-bye, Billy," she murmured faintly. "You're millions of miles away and you won't even twinkle once. But you kept where I could see you most of the time up there when there wasn't anything else but darkness to look at, didn't you? . . . Millions of miles . . . Good-bye, Billy Jackson."

Clara, the coloured maid, found the door locked at 10 the next day, and they forced it open. Vinegar, and the slapping of wrists and burnt feathers proving of no avail, some one ran to 'phone for an ambulance.

In due time it backed up to the door with much gong-clanging, and the capable young medico, in his white linen coat, ready, active, confident, with his smooth face half debonair, half grim, danced up the steps.

"Ambulance call to 49," he said briefly. "What's the trouble?"

"Oh, yes, doctor," sniffed Mrs. Parker, as though her trouble that there should be trouble in the house was the greater. "I can't think what can be the matter with her. Nothing we could do would bring her to. It's a young woman, a Miss Elsie—yes, a Miss Elsie Leeson. Never before in my house—"

"What room?" cried the doctor in a terrible voice, to which Mrs. Parker was a stranger.

"The skylight room. It—"

Evidently the ambulance doctor was familiar with the location of skylight rooms. He was gone up the stairs, four at a time. Mrs. Parker followed slowly, as her dignity demanded.

On the first landing she met him coming back bearing the astronomer in his arms. He stopped and let loose the practised scalpel of his tongue, not loudly. Gradually Mrs. Parker crumpled as a stiff garment that slips down from a nail. Ever afterward there remained crumples in her mind and body. Sometimes her curious roomers would ask her what the doctor said to her.

"Let that be," she would answer. "If I can get forgiveness for having heard it I will be satisfied."

The ambulance physician strode with his burden through the pack of hounds that follow the curiosity chase, and even they fell back along the sidewalk abashed, for his face was that of one who bears his own dead.

They noticed that he did not lay down upon the bed prepared for it in the ambulance the form that he carried, and all that he said was: "Drive like h——l, Wilson," to the driver.

That is all. Is it a story? In the next morning's paper I saw a little news item, and the last sentence of it may help you (as it helped me) to weld the incidents together.

It recounted the reception into Bellevue Hospital of a young woman who had been removed from No. 49 East ——street, suffering from debility induced by starvation. It concluded with these words:

"Dr. William Jackson, the ambulance physician who attended the case, says the patient will recover."

A Service of Love

WHEN one loves one's Art no service seems too hard. That is our premise. This story shall draw a conclusion from it, and show at the same time that the premise is incorrect. That will be a new thing in logic, and a feat in story-telling somewhat older than the great wall of China.

Joe Larrabee came out of the post-oak flats of the Middle West pulsing with a genius for pictorial art. At six he drew a picture of the town pump with a prominent citizen passing it hastily. This effort was framed and hung in the drug store window by the side of the ear of corn with an uneven number of rows. At twenty he left for New York with a flowing necktie and a capital tied up somewhat closer.

Delia Caruthers did things in six octaves so promisingly in a pine-tree village in the South that her relatives chipped in enough in her chip hat for her to go "North" and "finish." They could not see her f—, but that is our story.

Joe and Delia met in an atelier where a number of art and music students had gathered to discuss chiaroscuro, Wagner, music, Rembrandt's works, pictures, Waldteufel, wall paper, Chopin and Oolong.

Joe and Delia became enamoured one of the other, or each of the other, as you please, and in a short time were married—for (see above), when one loves one's Art no service seems too hard.

Mr. and Mrs. Larrabee began housekeeping in a flat. It was a lonesome flat—something like the A sharp way down at the left-hand end of the keyboard. And they were happy; for they had their Art, and they had each other. And my advice to the rich young man would be—sell all thou hast, and give it to the poor—janitor for the privilege of living in a flat with your Art and your Delia.

Flat-dwellers shall indorse my dictum that theirs is the only true happiness. If a home is happy it cannot fit too close—let the dresser collapse and become a billiard table; let the mantel turn to a rowing machine, the escritoire to a spare bedchamber, the washstand to an upright piano; let the four walls come together, if they will, so you and your Delia are between. But if home be the other kind, let it be wide and long—enter you at the Golden Gate, hang your hat on Hatteras, your cape on Cape Horn and go out by the Labrador.

Joe was painting in the class of the great Magister—you know his fame. His fees are high; his lessons are light—his high-lights have brought him renown. Delia was studying under Rosenstock—you know his repute as a disturber of the piano keys.

They were mighty happy as long as their money lasted. So is every—but I will not be cynical. Their aims were very clear and defined. Joe was to become capable very soon of turning out pictures that old gentlemen with thin side-whiskers and thick pocketbooks would sandbag one another in his studio for the privilege of buying. Delia was to become familiar and then contemptuous with Music, so that when she saw the orchestra seats and boxes unsold she could have sore throat and lobster in a private dining-room and refuse to go on the stage.

But the best, in my opinion, was the home life in the little flat—the ardent, voluble chats after the day's study; the cozy dinners and fresh, light breakfasts; the interchange of ambitions—ambitions interwoven each with the other's or else inconsiderable—the mutual help and inspiration; and—overlook my artlessness—stuffed olives and cheese sandwiches at 11 p.m.

But after a while Art flagged. It sometimes does, even if some switchman doesn't flag it. Everything going out and nothing coming in, as the vulgarians say. Money was lacking to pay Mr. Magister and Herr Rosenstock their prices. When one loves one's Art no service seems too hard. So, Delia said she must give music lessons to keep the chafing dish bubbling.

For two or three days she went out canvassing for pupils. One evening she came home elated.

"Joe, dear," she said, gleefully, "I've a pupil. And, oh, the loveliest people! General—General A. B. Pinkney's daughter—on Seventy-first street. Such a splendid house, Joe—you ought to see the front door! Byzantine I think you would call it. And inside! Oh, Joe, I never saw anything like it before.

"My pupil is his daughter Clementina. I dearly love her already. She's a delicate thing—dresses always in white; and the sweetest, simplest manners! Only eighteen years old. I'm to give three lessons a week; and, just think, Joe! $5 a lesson. I don't mind it a bit; for when I get two or three more pupils I can resume my lessons with Herr Rosenstock. Now, smooth out that wrinkle between your brows, dear, and let's have a nice supper."

"That's all right for you, Dele," said Joe, attacking a can of peas with a carving knife and a hatchet, "but how about me? Do you think I'm going to let you hustle for wages while I philander in the regions of high art? Not by the bones of Benvenuto Cellini! I guess I can sell papers or lay cobblestones, and bring in a dollar or two."

Delia came and hung about his neck.

"Joe, dear, you are silly. You must keep on at your studies. It is not as if I had quit my music and gone to work at something else. While I teach I learn. I am always with my music. And we can live as happily as millionaires on $15 a week. You mustn't think of leaving Mr. Magister."

"All right," said Joe, reaching for the blue scalloped vegetable dish. "But I hate for you to be giving lessons. It isn't Art. But you're a trump and a dear to do it."

"When one loves one's Art no service seems too hard," said Delia.

"Magister praised the sky in that sketch I made in the park," said Joe. "And Tinkle gave me permission to hang two of them in his window. I may sell one if the right kind of a moneyed idiot sees them."

"I'm sure you will," said Delia, sweetly. "And now let's be thankful for Gen. Pinkney and this veal roast."

During all of the next week the Larrabees had an early breakfast. Joe was enthusiastic about some morning-effect sketches he was doing in Central Park, and Delia packed him off breakfasted, coddled, praised and kissed at 7 o'clock. Art is an engaging mistress. It was most times 7 o'clock when he returned in the evening.

At the end of the week Delia, sweetly proud but languid, triumphantly tossed three five-dollar bills on the 8×10 (inches) centre table of the 8×10 (feet) flat parlour.

"Sometimes," she said, a little wearily, "Clementina tries me. I'm afraid she doesn't practise enough, and I have to tell her the same things so often. And then she always dresses entirely in white, and that does get monotonous. But Gen. Pinkney is the dearest old man! I wish you could know him, Joe. He comes in sometimes when I am with Clementina at the piano—he is a widower, you know—and stands there pulling his white goatee. 'And how are the semiquavers and the demisemiquavers progressing?' he always asks.

"I wish you could see the wainscoting in that drawing-room, Joe! And those Astrakhan rug portières. And Clementina has such a funny little cough. I hope she is stronger than she looks. Oh, I really am getting attached to her, she is so gentle and high bred. Gen. Pinkney's brother was once Minister to Bolivia."

And then Joe, with the air of a Monte Cristo, drew forth a ten, a five, a two and a one—all legal tender notes—and laid them beside Delia's earnings.

"Sold that watercolour of the obelisk to a man from Peoria," he announced overwhelmingly.

"Don't joke with me," said Delia, "not from Peoria!"

"All the way. I wish you could see him, Dele. Fat man with a woollen muffler and a quill toothpick. He saw the sketch in Tinkle's window and thought it was a windmill at first. He was game, though, and bought it anyhow. He ordered another—an oil sketch of the Lackawanna freight depot—to take back with him. Music lessons! Oh, I guess Art is still in it."

"I'm so glad you've kept on," said Delia, heartily. "You're bound to win, dear. Thirty-three dollars! We never had so much to spend before. We'll have oysters to-night."

"And filet mignon with champignons," said Joe. "Where is the olive fork?"

On the next Saturday evening Joe reached home first. He spread his $18 on the parlour table and washed what seemed to be a great deal of dark paint from his hands.

Half an hour later Delia arrived, her right hand tied up in a shapeless bundle of wraps and bandages.

"How is this?" asked Joe after the usual greetings. Delia laughed, but not very joyously.

"Clementina," she explained, "insisted upon a Welsh rabbit after her lesson. She is such a queer girl. Welsh rabbits at 5 in the afternoon. The General was there. You should have seen him run for the chafing dish, Joe, just as if there wasn't a servant in the house. I know Clementina isn't in good health; she is so nervous. In serving the rabbit she spilled a great lot of it, boiling hot, over my hand and wrist. It hurt awfully, Joe.

And the dear girl was so sorry! But Gen. Pinkney!—Joe, that old man nearly went distracted. He rushed downstairs and sent somebody—they said the furnace man or somebody in the basement—out to a drug store for some oil and things to bind it up with. It doesn't hurt so much now."

"What's this?" asked Joe, taking the hand tenderly and pulling at some white strands beneath the bandages.

"It's something soft," said Delia, "that had oil on it. Oh, Joe, did you sell another sketch?" She had seen the money on the table.

"Did I?" said Joe; "just ask the man from Peoria. He got his depot to-day, and he isn't sure but he thinks he wants another parkscape and a view on the Hudson. What time this afternoon did you burn your hand, Dele?"

"Five o'clock, I think," said Dele, plaintively. "The iron—I mean the rabbit came off the fire about that time. You ought to have seen Gen. Pinkney, Joe, when—"

"Sit down here a moment, Dele," said Joe. He drew her to the couch, sat beside her and put his arm across her shoulders.

"What have you been doing for the last two weeks, Dele?" he asked.

She braved it for a moment or two with an eye full of love and stubbornness, and murmured a phrase or two vaguely of Gen. Pinkney; but at length down went her head and out came the truth and tears.

"I couldn't get any pupils," she confessed. "And I couldn't bear to have you give up your lessons; and I got a place ironing shirts in that big Twenty-fourth street laundry. And I think I did very well to make up both General Pinkney and Clementina, don't you, Joe? And when a girl in the laundry set down a hot iron on my hand this afternoon I was all the way home making up that story about the Welsh rabbit. You're not angry, are you, Joe? And if I hadn't got the work you mightn't have sold your sketches to that man from Peoria."

"He wasn't from Peoria," said Joe, slowly.

"Well, it doesn't matter where he was from. How clever you are, Joe—and—kiss me, Joe—and what made you ever suspect that I wasn't giving music lessons to Clementina?"

"I didn't," said Joe, "until to-night. And I wouldn't have then, only I sent up this cotton waste and oil from the engine-room this afternoon for a girl upstairs who had her hand burned with a smoothing-iron. I've been firing the engine in that laundry for the last two weeks."

"And then you didn't—"

"My purchaser from Peoria," said Joe, "and Gen. Pinkney are both creations of the same art—but you wouldn't call it either painting or music."

And then they both laughed, and Joe began:

"When one loves one's Art no service seems—"

But Delia stopped him with her hand on his lips. "No," she said—"just 'When one loves.'"

The Coming Out of Maggie

EVERY Saturday night the Clover Leaf Social Club gave a hop in the hall of the Give and Take Athletic Association on the East Side. In order to attend one of these dances you must be a member of the Give and Take—or, if you belong to the division that starts off with the right foot in waltzing, you must work in Rhinegold's paper-box factory. Still, any Clover Leaf was privileged to escort or be escorted by an outsider to a single dance. But mostly each Give and Take brought the paper-box girl that he affected; and few strangers could boast of having shaken a foot at the regular hops.

Maggie Toole, on account of her dull eyes, broad mouth and left-handed style of footwork in the two-step, went to the dances with Anna McCarty and her "fellow." Anna and Maggie worked side by side in the factory, and were the greatest chums ever. So Anna always made Jimmy Burns take her by Maggie's house every Saturday night so that her friend could go to the dance with them.

The Give and Take Athletic Association lived up to its name. The hall of the association in Orchard street was fitted out with muscle-making inventions. With the fibres thus builded up the members were wont to engage the police and rival social and athletic organisations in joyous combat. Between these more serious occupations the Saturday night hop with the paper-box factory girls came as a refining influence and as an efficient screen. For sometimes the tip went 'round, and if you were among the elect that tiptoed up the dark back stairway you might see as neat and satisfying a little welter-weight affair to a finish as ever happened inside the ropes.

On Saturdays Rhinegold's paper-box factory closed at 3 P. M. On one such afternoon Anna and Maggie walked homeward together. At Maggie's door Anna said, as usual: "Be ready at seven, sharp, Mag; and Jimmy and me'll come by for you."

But what was this? Instead of the customary humble and grateful thanks from the non-escorted one there was to be perceived a high-poised head, a prideful dimpling at the corners of a broad mouth, and almost a sparkle in a dull brown eye.

"Thanks, Anna," said Maggie; "but you and Jimmy needn't bother to-night. I've a gentleman friend that's coming 'round to escort me to the hop."

The comely Anna pounced upon her friend, shook her, chided and beseeched her. Maggie Toole catch a fellow! Plain, dear, loyal, unattractive Maggie, so sweet as a chum, so unsought for a two-step or a moonlit bench in the little park. How was it? When did it happen? Who was it?

"You'll see to-night," said Maggie, flushed with the wine of the first grapes she had gathered in Cupid's vineyard. "He's swell all right. He's two inches taller than Jimmy, and an up-to-date dresser. I'll introduce him, Anna, just as soon as we get to the hall."

Anna and Jimmy were among the first Clover Leafs to arrive that evening. Anna's eyes were brightly fixed upon the door of the hall to catch the first glimpse of her friend's "catch."

At 8:30 Miss Toole swept into the hall with her escort. Quickly her triumphant eye discovered her chum under the wing of her faithful Jimmy.

"Oh, gee!" cried Anna, "Mag ain't made a hit—oh, no! Swell fellow? well, I guess! Style? Look at 'um."

"Go as far as you like," said Jimmy, with sandpaper in his voice. "Cop him out if you want him. These new guys always win out with the push. Don't mind me. He don't squeeze all the limes, I guess. Huh!"

"Shut up, Jimmy. You know what I mean. I'm glad for Mag. First fellow she ever had. Oh, here they come."

Across the floor Maggie sailed like a coquettish yacht convoyed by a stately cruiser. And truly, her companion justified the encomiums of the faithful chum. He stood two inches taller than the average Give and Take athlete; his dark hair curled; his eyes and his teeth flashed whenever he bestowed his frequent smiles. The young men of the Clover Leaf Club pinned not their faith to the graces of person as much as they did to its prowess, its achievements in hand-to-hand conflicts, and its preservation from the legal duress that constantly menaced it. The member of the association who would bind a paper-box maiden to his conquering chariot scorned to employ Beau Brummel airs. They were not considered honourable methods of warfare. The swelling biceps, the coat straining at its buttons over the chest, the air of conscious conviction of the supereminence of the male in the cosmogony of creation, even a calm display of bow legs as subduing and enchanting agents in the gentle tourneys of Cupid—these were the approved arms and ammunition of the Clover Leaf gallants. They viewed, then, genuflexions and alluring poses of this visitor with their chins at a new angle.

"A friend of mine, Mr. Terry O'Sullivan," was Maggie's formula of introduction. She led him around the room, presenting him to each new-arriving Clover Leaf. Almost was she pretty now, with the unique luminosity in her eyes that comes to a girl with her first suitor and a kitten with its first mouse.

"Maggie Toole's got a fellow at last," was the word that went round among the paper-box girls. "Pipe Mag's floor-walker"—thus the Give and Takes expressed their indifferent contempt.

Usually at the weekly hops Maggie kept a spot on the wall warm with her back. She felt and showed so much gratitude whenever a self-sacrificing partner invited her to dance that his pleasure was cheapened and diminished. She had even grown used to noticing Anna joggle the reluctant Jimmy with her elbow as a signal for him to invite her chum to walk over his feet through a two-step.

But to-night the pumpkin had turned to a coach and six. Terry O'Sullivan was a victorious Prince Charming, and Maggie Toole winged her first butterfly flight. And though our tropes of fairyland be mixed with those of entomology they shall not spill one drop of ambrosia from the rose-crowned melody of Maggie's one perfect night.

The girls besieged her for introductions to her "fellow." The Clover Leaf young men, after two years of blindness, suddenly perceived charms in Miss Toole. They flexed their compelling muscles before her and bespoke her for the dance.

Thus she scored; but to Terry O'Sullivan the honours of the evening fell thick and fast. He shook his curls; he smiled and went easily through the seven motions for acquiring grace in your own room before an open window ten minutes each day. He danced like a faun; he introduced manner and style and atmosphere; his words came trippingly upon his tongue, and—he waltzed twice in succession with the paper-box girl that Dempsey Donovan brought.

Dempsey was the leader of the association. He wore a dress suit, and could chin the bar twice with one hand. He was one of "Big Mike" O'Sullivan's lieutenants, and was never troubled by trouble. No cop dared to arrest him. Whenever he broke a pushcart man's head or shot a member of the Heinrick B. Sweeney Outing and Literary Association in the kneecap, an officer would drop around and say:

"The Cap'n 'd like to see ye a few minutes round to the office whin ye have time, Dempsey, me boy."

But there would be sundry gentlemen there with large

gold fob chains and black cigars; and somebody would tell a funny story, and then Dempsey would go back and work half an hour with the six-pound dumbbells. So, doing a tight-rope act on a wire stretched across Niagara was a safe terpsichorean performance compared with waltzing twice with Dempsey Donovan's paper-box girl. At 10 o'clock the jolly round face of "Big Mike" O'Sullivan shone at the door for five minutes upon the scene. He always looked in for five minutes, smiled at the girls and handed out real perfectos to the delighted boys.

Dempsey Donovan was at his elbow instantly, talking rapidly. "Big Mike" looked carefully at the dancers, smiled, shook his head and departed.

The music stopped. The dancers scattered to the chairs along the walls. Terry O'Sullivan, with his entrancing bow, relinquished a pretty girl in blue to her partner and started back to find Maggie. Dempsey intercepted him in the middle of the floor.

Some fine instinct that Rome must have bequeathed to us caused nearly every one to turn and look at them—there was a subtle feeling that two gladiators had met in the arena. Two or three Give and Takes with tight coat sleeves drew nearer.

"One moment, Mr. O'Sullivan," said Dempsey. "I hope you're enjoying yourself. Where did you say you live?"

The two gladiators were well matched. Dempsey had, perhaps, ten pounds of weight to give away. The O'Sullivan had breadth with quickness. Dempsey had a glacial eye, a dominating slit of a mouth, an indestructible jaw, a complexion like a belle's and the coolness of a champion. The visitor showed more fire in his contempt and less control over his conspicuous sneer. They were enemies by the law written when the rocks were molten. They were each too splendid, too mighty, too incomparable to divide pre-eminence. One only must survive.

"I live on Grand," said O'Sullivan, insolently; "and no trouble to find me at home. Where do you live?"

Dempsey ignored the question.

"You say your name's O'Sullivan," he went on. "Well, 'Big Mike' says he never saw you before."

"Lots of things he never saw," said the favourite of the hop.

"As a rule," went on Dempsey, huskily sweet, "O'Sullivans in this district know one another. You escorted one of our lady members here, and we want a chance to make good. If you've got a family tree let's see a few historical O'Sullivan buds come out on it. Or do you want us to dig it out of you by the roots?"

"Suppose you mind your own business," suggested O'Sullivan, blandly.

Dempsey's eye brightened. He held up an inspired forefinger as though a brilliant idea had struck him.

"I've got it now," he said cordially. "It was just a little mistake. You ain't no O'Sullivan. You are a ring-tailed monkey. Excuse us for not recognising you at first."

O'Sullivan's eye flashed. He made a quick movement, but Andy Geoghan was ready and caught his arm.

Dempsey nodded at Andy and William McMahan, the secretary of the club, and walked rapidly toward a door at the rear of the hall. Two other members of the Give and Take Association swiftly joined the little group. Terry O'Sullivan was now in the hands of the Board of Rules and Social Referees. They spoke to him briefly and softly, and conducted him out through the same door at the rear.

This movement on the part of the Clover Leaf members requires a word of elucidation. Back of the association hall was a smaller room rented by the club. In this room personal difficulties that arose on the ballroom floor were settled, man to man, with the weapons of nature, under the supervision of the board. No lady could say that she had witnessed a fight at a Clover Leaf hop in several years. Its gentlemen members guaranteed that.

So easily and smoothly had Dempsey and the board done their preliminary work that many in the hall had not noticed the checking of the fascinating O'Sullivan's social triumph. Among these was Maggie. She looked about for her escort.

"Smoke up!" said Rose Cassidy. "Wasn't you on? Demps Donovan picked a scrap with your Lizzie-boy, and they've waltzed out to the slaughter room with him. How's my hair look done up this way, Mag?"

Maggie laid a hand on the bosom of her cheesecloth waist.

"Gone to fight with Dempsey!" she said, breathlessly. "They've got to be stopped. Dempsey Donovan can't fight him. Why, he'll—he'll kill him!"

"Ah, what do you care?" said Rosa. "Don't some of 'em fight every hop?"

But Maggie was off, darting her zig-zag way through the maze of dancers. She burst through the rear door into the dark hall and then threw her solid shoulder against the door of the room of single combat. It gave way, and in the instant that she entered her eye caught the scene—the Board standing about with open watches; Dempsey Donovan in his shirt sleeves dancing, light-footed, with the wary grace of the modern pugilist, within easy reach of his adversary; Terry O'Sullivan standing with arms folded and a murderous look in his dark eyes. And without slacking the speed of her entrance she leaped forward with a scream—leaped in time to catch and hang upon the arm of O'Sullivan that was suddenly uplifted, and to whisk from it the long, bright stiletto that he had drawn from his bosom.

The knife fell and rang upon the floor. Cold steel drawn in the rooms of the Give and Take Association! Such a thing had never happened before. Every one stood motionless for a minute. Andy Geoghan kicked the stiletto with the toe of his shoe curiously, like an antiquarian who has come upon some ancient weapon unknown to his learning.

And then O'Sullivan hissed something unintelligible between his teeth. Dempsey and the board exchanged looks. And then Dempsey looked at O'Sullivan without anger, as one looks at a stray dog, and nodded his head in the direction of the door.

"The back stairs, Giuseppi," he said, briefly. "Somebody'll pitch your hat down after you."

Maggie walked up to Dempsey Donovan. There was a brilliant spot of red in her cheeks, down which slow tears were running. But she looked him bravely in the eye.

"I knew it, Dempsey," she said, as her eyes grew dull even in their tears. "I knew he was a Guinea. His name's Tony Spinelli. I hurried in when they told me you and him was scrappin'. Them Guineas always carries knives. But you don't understand, Dempsey. I never had a fellow in my life. I got tired of comin' with Anna and Jimmy every night, so I fixed it with him to call himself O'Sullivan, and brought him along. I knew there'd be nothin' doin' for him if he came as a Dago. I guess I'll resign from the club now."

Dempsey turned to Andy Geoghan.

"Chuck that cheese slicer out of the window," he said, "and tell 'em inside that Mr. O'Sullivan has had a telephone message to go down to Tammany Hall."

And then he turned back to Maggie.

"Say, Mag," he said, "I'll see you home. And how about next Saturday night? Will you come to the hop with me if I call around for you?"

It was remarkable how quickly Maggie's eyes could change from dull to a shining brown.

"With you, Dempsey?" she stammered. "Say—will a duck swim?"

After Twenty Years

THE policeman on the beat moved up the avenue impressively. The impressiveness was habitual and not for show, for spectators were few. The time was barely 10 o'clock at night, but chilly gusts of wind with a taste of rain in them had well nigh de-peopled the streets.

Trying doors as he went, twirling his club with many intricate and artful movements, turning now and then to cast his watchful eye adown the pacific thoroughfare, the officer, with his stalwart form and slight swagger, made a fine picture of a guardian of the peace. The vicinity was one that kept early hours. Now and then you might see the lights of a cigar store or of an all-night lunch counter; but the majority of the doors belonged to business places that had long since been closed.

When about midway of a certain block the policeman suddenly slowed his walk. In the doorway of a darkened hardware store a man leaned, with an unlighted cigar in his mouth. As the policeman walked up to him the man spoke up quickly.

"It's all right, officer," he said, reassuringly. "I'm just waiting for a friend. It's an appointment made twenty years ago. Sounds a little funny to you, doesn't it? Well, I'll explain if you'd like to make certain it's all straight. About that long ago there used to be a restaurant where this store stands—'Big Joe' Brady's restaurant."

"Until five years ago," said the policeman. "It was torn down then."

The man in the doorway struck a match and lit his cigar. The light showed a pale, square-jawed face with keen eyes, and a little white scar near his right eyebrow. His scarfpin was a large diamond, oddly set.

"Twenty years ago to-night," said the man, "I dined here at 'Big Joe' Brady's with Jimmy Wells, my best chum, and the finest chap in the world. He and I were raised here in New York, just like two brothers, together. I was eighteen and Jimmy was twenty. The next morning I was to start for the West to make my fortune. You couldn't have dragged Jimmy out of New York; he thought it was the only place on earth. Well, we agreed that night that we would meet here again exactly twenty years from that date and time, no matter what our conditions might be or from what distance we might have to come. We figured that in twenty years each of us ought to have our destiny worked out and our fortunes made, whatever they were going to be."

"It sounds pretty interesting," said the policeman. "Rather a long time between meets, though, it seems to me. Haven't you heard from your friend since you left?"

"Well, yes, for a time we corresponded," said the other. "But after a year or two we lost track of each other. You see, the West is a pretty big proposition, and I kept hustling around over it pretty lively. But I know Jimmy will meet me here if he's alive, for he always was the truest, stanchest old chap in the world. He'll never forget. I came a thousand miles to stand in this door to-night, and it's worth it if my old partner turns up."

The waiting man pulled out a handsome watch, the lids of it set with small diamonds.

"Three minutes to ten," he announced. "It was exactly ten o'clock when we parted here at the restaurant door."

"Did pretty well out West, didn't you?" asked the policeman.

"You bet! I hope Jimmy has done half as well. He was a kind of plodder, though, good fellow as he was. I've had to compete with some of the sharpest wits going to get my pile.

A man gets in a groove in New York. It takes the West to put a razor-edge on him."

The policeman twirled his club and took a step or two.

"I'll be on my way. Hope your friend comes around all right. Going to call time on him sharp?"

"I should say not!" said the other. "I'll give him half an hour at least. If Jimmy is alive on earth he'll be here by that time. So long, officer."

"Good-night, sir," said the policeman, passing on along his beat, trying doors as he went.

There was now a fine, cold drizzle falling, and the wind had risen from its uncertain puffs into a steady blow. The few foot passengers astir in that quarter hurried dismally and silently along with coat collars turned high and pocketed hands. And in the door of the hardware store the man who had come a thousand miles to fill an appointment, uncertain almost to absurdity, with the friend of his youth, smoked his cigar and waited.

About twenty minutes he waited, and then a tall man in a long overcoat, with collar turned up to his ears, hurried across from the opposite side of the street. He went directly to the waiting man.

"Is that you, Bob?" he asked, doubtfully.

"Is that you, Jimmy Wells?" cried the man in the door.

"Bless my heart!" exclaimed the new arrival, grasping both the other's hands with his own. "It's Bob, sure as fate. I was certain I'd find you here if you were still in existence. Well, well, well!—twenty years is a long time. The old restaurant's gone, Bob; I wish it had lasted, so we could have had another dinner there. How has the West treated you, old man?"

"Bully; it has given me everything I asked it for. You've changed lots, Jimmy. I never thought you were so tall by two or three inches."

"Oh, I grew a bit after I was twenty."

"Doing well in New York, Jimmy?"

"Moderately. I have a position in one of the city departments. Come on, Bob; we'll go around to a place I know of, and have a good long talk about old times."

The two men started up the street, arm in arm. The man from the West, his egotism enlarged by success, was beginning to outline the history of his career. The other, submerged in his overcoat, listened with interest.

At the corner stood a drug store, brilliant with electric lights. When they came into this glare each of them turned simultaneously to gaze upon the other's face.

The man from the West stopped suddenly and released his arm.

"You're not Jimmy Wells," he snapped. "Twenty years is a long time, but not long enough to change a man's nose from a Roman to a pug."

"It sometimes changes a good man into a bad one," said the tall man. "You've been under arrest for ten minutes, 'Silky' Bob. Chicago thinks you may have dropped over our way and wires us she wants to have a chat with you. Going quietly, are you? That's sensible. Now, before we go on to the station here's a note I was asked to hand you. You may read it here at the window. It's from Patrolman Wells."

The man from the West unfolded the little piece of paper handed him. His hand was steady when he began to read, but it trembled a little by the time he had finished. The note was rather short.

Bob: I was at the appointed place on time. When you struck the match to light your cigar I saw it was the face of the man wanted in Chicago. Somehow I couldn't do it myself, so I went around and got a plain clothes man to do the job.

JIMMY.

A Night in New Arabia

THE great city of Bagdad-on-the-Subway is caliph-ridden. Its palaces, bazaars, khans, and byways are thronged with Al Rashids in divers disguises, seeking diversion and victims for their unbridled generosity. You can scarcely find a poor beggar whom they are willing to let enjoy his spoils unsuccored, nor a wrecked unfortunate upon whom they will not reshower the means of fresh misfortune. You will hardly find anywhere a hungry one who has not had the opportunity to tighten his belt in gift libraries, nor a poor pundit who has not blushed at the holiday basket of celery-crowned turkey forced resoundingly through his door by the eleemosynary press.

So then, fearfully through the Harun-haunted streets creep the one-eyed calenders, the Little Hunchback and the Barber's Sixth Brother, hoping to escape the ministrations of the roving horde of caliphoid sultans.

Entertainment for many Arabian nights might be had from the histories of those who have escaped the largesse of the army of Commanders of the Faithful. Until dawn you might sit on the enchanted rug and listen to such stories as are told of the powerful genie Roc-Ef-El-Er who sent the Forty Thieves to soak up the oil plant of Ali Baba; of the good Caliph Kar-Neg-Ghe, who gave away palaces; of the Seven Voyages of Sailbad, the Sinner, who frequented wooden excursion steamers among the islands; of the Fisherman and the Bottle; of the Barmecides' Boarding house; of Aladdin's rise to wealth by means of his Wonderful Gas-meter.

But now, there being ten sultans to one Sheherazade, she is held too valuable to be in fear of the bowstring. In consequence the art of narrative languishes. And, as the lesser caliphs are hunting the happy poor and the resigned unfortunate from cover to cover in order to heap upon them strange mercies and mysterious benefits, too often comes the report from Arabian headquarters that the captive refused "to talk."

This reticence, then, in the actors who perform the sad comedies of their philanthropy-scourged world, must, in a degree, account for the shortcomings of this painfully gleaned tale, which shall be called

THE STORY OF THE CALIPH WHO ALLEVIATED HIS CONSCIENCE

Old Jacob Spraggins mixed for himself some Scotch and lithia water at his $1,200 oak sideboard. Inspiration must have resulted from its imbibition, for immediately afterward he struck the quartered oak soundly with his fist and shouted to the empty dining room:

"By the coke ovens of hell, it must be that ten thousand dollars! If I can get that squared, it'll do the trick."

Thus, by the commonest artifice of the trade, having gained your interest, the action of the story will now be suspended, leaving you grumpily to consider a sort of dull biography beginning fifteen years before.

When old Jacob was young Jacob he was a breaker boy in a Pennsylvania coal mine. I don't know what a breaker boy is; but his occupation seems to be standing by a coal dump with a wan look and a dinner-pail to have his picture taken for magazine articles. Anyhow, Jacob was one. But, instead of dying of overwork at nine, and leaving his helpless parents and brothers at the mercy of the union strikers' reserve fund, he hitched up his galluses, put a dollar or two in a side proposition now and then, and at forty-five was worth $20,000,000.

There now! it's over. Hardly had time to yawn, did you? I've seen biographies that—but let us dissemble.

I want you to consider Jacob Spraggins, Esq., after he had arrived at the seventh stage of his career. The stages meant are, first, humble origin; second, deserved promotion; third, stockholder; fourth, capitalist; fifth, trust magnate; sixth, rich malefactor; seventh, caliph; eighth, x. The eighth stage shall be left to the higher mathematics.

At fifty-five Jacob retired from active business. The income of a czar was still rolling in on him from coal, iron, real estate, oil, railroads, manufactories, and corporations, but none of it touched Jacob's hands in a raw state. It was a sterilized increment, carefully cleaned and dusted and fumigated until it arrived at its ultimate stage of untainted, spotless checks in the white fingers of his private secretary. Jacob built a three-million-dollar palace on a corner lot fronting on Nabob Avenue, city of New Bagdad, and began to feel the mantle of the late H. A. Rashid descending upon him. Eventually Jacob slipped the mantle under his collar, tied it in a neat four-in-hand, and became a licensed harrier of our Mesopotamian proletariat.

When a man's income becomes so large that the butcher actually sends him the kind of steak he orders, he begins to think about his soul's salvation. Now, the various stages or classes of rich men must not be forgotten. The capitalist can tell you to a dollar the amount of his wealth. The trust magnate "estimates" it. The rich malefactor hands you a cigar and denies that he has bought the P. D. & Q. The caliph merely smiles and talks about Hammerstein and the musical lasses. There is a record of tremendous altercation at breakfast in a "Where-to-Dine-Well" tavern between a magnate and his wife, the rift within the loot being that the wife calculated their fortune at a figure $3,000,000 higher than did her future *divorcé*. Oh, well, I, myself, heard a similar quarrel between a man and his wife because he found fifty cents less in his pockets than he thought he had. After all, we are all human—Count Tolstoi, R. Fitzsimmons, Peter Pan, and the rest of us.

Don't lose heart because the story seems to be degenerating into a sort of moral essay for intellectual readers.

There will be dialogue and stage business pretty soon.

When Jacob first began to compare the eyes of needles with the camels in the Zoo he decided upon organized charity. He had his secretary send a check for one million to the Universal Benevolent Association of the Globe. You may have looked down through a grating in front of a decayed warehouse for a nickel that you had dropped through. But that is neither here nor there. The Association acknowledged receipt of his favor of the 24th ult. with enclosure as stated. Separated by a double line, but still mighty close to the matter under the caption of "Oddities of the Day's News" in an evening paper, Jacob Spraggins read that one "Jasper Spargyous" had "donated $100,000 to the U. B. A. of G." A camel may have a stomach for each day in the week; but I dare not venture to accord him whiskers, for fear of the Great Displeasure at Washington; but if he have whiskers, surely not one of them will seem to have been inserted in the eye of a needle by that effort of that rich man to enter the K. of H. The right is reserved to reject any and all bids; signed, S. Peter, secretary and gatekeeper.

Next, Jacob selected the best endowed college he could scare up and presented it with a $200,000 laboratory. The college did not maintain a scientific course, but it accepted the money and built an elaborate lavatory instead, which was no diversion of funds so far as Jacob ever discovered.

The faculty met and invited Jacob to come over and take his A B C degree. Before sending the invitation they smiled, cut out the C, added the proper punctuation marks, and all was well.

While walking on the campus before being capped and gowned, Jacob saw two professors strolling nearby. Their voices, long adapted to indoor acoustics, undesignedly reached his ear.

"There goes the latest *chevalier d'industrie*," said one of them, "to buy a sleeping powder from us. He gets his degree to-morrow."

"*In foro conscientiæ*," said the other. "Let's 'eave 'arf a brick at 'im."

Jacob ignored the Latin, but the brick pleasantry was not too hard for him. There was no mandragora in the honorary draught of learning that he had bought. That was before the passage of the Pure Food and Drugs Act.

Jacob wearied of philanthropy on a large scale.

"If I could see folks made happier," he said to himself—"If I could see 'em myself and hear 'em express their gratitude for what I done for 'em it would make me feel better. This donatin' funds to institutions and societies is about as satisfactory as dropping money into a broken slot machine."

So Jacob followed his nose, which led him through unswept streets to the homes of the poorest.

"The very thing!" said Jacob. "I will charter two river steamboats, pack them full of these unfortunate children and—say ten thousand dolls and drums and a thousand freezers of ice cream, and give them a delightful outing up the Sound. The sea breezes on that trip ought to blow the taint off some of this money that keeps coming in faster than I can work it off my mind."

Jacob must have leaked some of his benevolent intentions, for an immense person with a bald face and a mouth that looked as if it ought to have a "Drop Letters Here" sign over it hooked a finger around him and set him in a space between a barber's pole and a stack of ash cans. Words came out of the post-office slit—smooth, husky words with gloves on 'em, but sounding as if they might turn to bare knuckles any moment.

"Say, Sport, do you know where you are at? Well, dis is Mike O'Grady's district you're buttin' into—see? Mike's got de stomach-ache privilege for every kid in dis neighborhood—see? And if dere's any picnics or red balloons to be dealt out here, Mike's money pays for 'em—see? Don't you butt in, or something'll be handed to you. Youse d—— settlers and reformers with your social ologies and your millionaire detectives have got dis district in a hell of a fix, anyhow. With your college students and professors rough-housing de soda-water stands and dem rubber-neck coaches fillin' de streets, de folks down here are 'fraid to go out of de houses. Now, you leave 'em to Mike. Dey belongs to him, and he knows how to handle 'em. Keep on your own side of de town. Are you some wiser now, uncle, or do you want to scrap wit' Mike O'Grady for de Santa Claus belt in dis district?"

Clearly, that spot in the moral vineyard was preempted. So Caliph Spraggins menaced no more the people in the bazaars of the East Side. To keep down his growing surplus he doubled his donations to organized charity, presented the Y. M. C. A. of his native town with a $10,000 collection of butterflies, and sent a check to the famine sufferers in China big enough to buy new emerald eyes and diamond-filled teeth for all their gods. But none of these charitable acts seemed to bring peace to the caliph's heart. He tried to get a personal note into his benefactions by tipping bellboys and waiters $10 and $20 bills. He got well snickered at and derided for that by the minions who accept with respect gratuities commensurate to the service performed. He sought out an ambitious and talented but poor young woman, and bought for her the star part in a new comedy. He might have gotten rid of $50,000 more of his cumbersome money in this philanthropy if he had not neglected to write letters to her. But she lost the suit for lack of evidence, while his capital still kept piling up, and his *optikos needleorum camelibus*—or rich man's disease—was unrelieved.

In Caliph Spraggins's $3,000,000 home lived his sister Henrietta, who used to cook for the coal miners in a twenty-five-cent eating house in Coketown, Pa., and who now would have offered John Mitchell only two fingers of her hand to shake. And his daughter Celia, nineteen, back from boarding-school and from being polished off by private instructors in the restaurant languages and those études and things.

Celia is the heroine. Lest the artist's delineation of her charms on this very page humbug your fancy, take from me her authorized description. She was a nice-looking, awkward, loud, rather bashful, brown-haired girl, with a sallow complexion, bright eyes, and a perpetual smile. She had a wholesome, Spraggins-inherited love for plain food, loose clothing, and the society of the lower classes. She had too much health and youth to feel the burden of wealth. She had a wide mouth that kept the peppermint-pepsin tablets rattling like hail from the slot-machine wherever she went, and she could whistle hornpipes. Keep this picture in mind; and let the artist do his worst.

Celia looked out of her window one day and gave her heart to the grocer's young man. The receiver thereof was at that moment engaged in conceding immortality to his horse and calling down upon him the ultimate fate of the wicked; so he did not notice the transfer. A horse should stand still when you are lifting a crate of strictly new-laid eggs out of the wagon.

Young lady reader, you would have liked that grocer's young man yourself. But you wouldn't have given him your heart, because you are saving it for a riding-master, or a shoe-manufacturer with a torpid liver, or something quiet but rich in gray tweeds at Palm Beach. Oh, I know about it. So I am glad the grocer's young man was for Celia, and not for you.

The grocer's young man was slim and straight and as confident and easy in his movements as the man in the back of the magazines who wears the new frictionless roller suspenders. He wore a gray bicycle cap on the back of his head, and his hair was straw-colored and curly, and his sunburned face looked like one that smiled a good deal when he was not preaching the doctrine of everlasting punishment to delivery-wagon horses. He slung imported A1 fancy groceries about as though they were only the stuff he delivered at boarding-houses; and when he picked up his whip, your mind instantly recalled Mr. Tackett and his air with the buttonless foils.

Tradesmen delivered their goods at a side gate at the rear of the house. The grocer's wagon came about ten in the morning. For three days Celia watched the driver when he came, finding something new each time to admire in the lofty and almost contemptuous way he had of tossing around the choicest gifts of Pomona, Ceres, and the canning factories. Then she consulted Annette.

To be explicit, Annette McCorkle, the second housemaid who deserves a paragraph herself. Annette Fletcherized large numbers of romantic novels which she obtained at a free public library branch (donated by one of the biggest caliphs in the business). She was Celia's side-kicker and chum, though Aunt Henrietta didn't know it, you may hazard a bean or two.

"Oh, canary-bird seed!" exclaimed Annette. "Ain't it a corkin' situation? You a heiress, and fallin' in love with him on sight! He's a sweet boy, too, and above his business. But he ain't susceptible like the common run of grocer's assistants. He never pays no attention to me."

"He will to me," said Celia.

"Riches—" began Annette, unsheathing the not unjustifiable feminine sting.

"Oh, you're not so beautiful," said Celia, with her wide, disarming smile. "Neither am I; but he sha'n't know that there's any money mixed up with my looks, such as they are. That's fair. Now, I want you to lend me one of your caps and an apron, Annette."

"Oh, marshmallows!" cried Annette. "I see. Ain't it lovely? It's just like 'Lurline, the Left-Handed; or, A Buttonhole Maker's Wrongs.' I'll bet he'll turn out to be a count."

There was a long hallway (or "passageway," as they call it in the land of the Colonels) with one side latticed, running along the rear of the house. The grocer's young man went through this to deliver his goods. One morning he passed a girl in there with shining eyes, sallow complexion, and wide, smiling mouth, wearing a maid's cap and apron. But as he was cumbered with a basket of Early Drumhead lettuce and Trophy tomatoes and three bunches of asparagus and six bottles of the most expensive Queen olives, he saw no more than that she was one of the maids.

But on his way out he came up behind her, and she was whistling "Fisher's Hornpipe" so loudly and clearly that all the piccolos in the world should have disjointed themselves and crept into their cases for shame.

The grocer's young man stopped and pushed back his cap until it hung on his collar button behind.

"That's out o' sight, Kid," said he.

"My name is Celia, if you please," said the whistler, dazzling him with a three-inch smile.

"That's all right. I'm Thomas McLeod. What part of the house do you work in?"

"I'm the—the second parlor maid."

"Do you know the 'Falling Waters'?"

"No," said Celia, "we don't know anybody. We got rich too quick—that is, Mr. Spraggins did."

"I'll make you acquainted," said Thomas McLeod. "It's a strathspey—the first cousin to a hornpipe."

If Celia's whistling put the piccolos out of commission, Thomas McLeod's surely made the biggest flutes hunt their holes. He could actually whistle *bass*.

When he stopped Celia was ready to jump into his delivery wagon and ride with him clear to the end of the pier and on to the ferry-boat of the Charon line.

"I'll be around to-morrow at 10:15," said Thomas, "with some spinach and a case of carbonic."

"I'll practice that what-you-may-call-it," said Celia. "I can whistle a fine second."

The processes of courtship are personal, and do not belong to general literature. They should be chronicled in detail only in advertisements of iron tonics and in the secret by-laws of the Woman's Auxiliary of the Ancient Order of the Rat Trap. But genteel writing may contain a description of certain stages of its progress without intruding upon the province of the X-ray or of park policemen.

A day came when Thomas McLeod and Celia lingered at the end of the latticed "passage."

"Sixteen a week isn't much," said Thomas, letting his cap rest on his shoulder blades.

Celia looked through the lattice-work and whistled a dead march. Shopping with Aunt Henrietta the day before, she had paid that much for a dozen handkerchiefs.

"Maybe I'll get a raise next month," said Thomas. "I'll be around to-morrow at the same time with a bag of flour and the laundry soap."

"All right," said Celia. "Annette's married cousin pays only $20 a month for a flat in the Bronx."

Never for a moment did she count on the Spraggins money. She knew Aunt Henrietta's invincible pride of caste and pa's mightiness as a Colossus of cash, and she understood that if she chose Thomas she and her grocer's young man might go whistle for a living.

Another day came, Thomas violating the dignity of Nabob Avenue with "The Devil's Dream," whistled keenly between his teeth.

"Raised to eighteen a week yesterday," he said. "Been pricing flats around Morningside. You want to start untying those apron strings and unpinning that cap, old girl."

"Oh, Tommy!" said Celia, with her broadest smile. "Won't that be enough? I got Betty to show me how to make a cottage pudding. I guess we could call it a flat pudding if we wanted to."

"And tell no lie," said Thomas.

"And I can sweep and polish and dust—of course, a parlor maid learns that. And we could whistle duets of evenings."

"The old man said he'd raise me to twenty at Christmas if Bryan couldn't think of any harder name to call a Republican than a 'postponer,'" said the grocer's young man.

"I can sew," said Celia; "and I know that you must make the gas company's man show his badge when he comes to look at the meter; and I know how to put up quince jam and window curtains."

"Bully! you're all right, Cele. Yes, I believe we can pull it off on eighteen."

As he was jumping into the wagon the second parlor maid braved discovery by running swiftly to the gate.

"And, oh, Tommy, I forgot," she called, softly. "I believe I could make your neckties."

"Forget it," said Thomas decisively.

"And another thing," she continued. "Sliced cucumbers at night will drive away cockroaches."

"And sleep, too, you bet," said Mr. McLeod. "Yes, I believe if I have a delivery to make on the West Side this afternoon I'll look in at a furniture store I know over there."

It was just as the wagon dashed away that old Jacob Spraggins struck the sideboard with his fist and made the mysterious remark about ten thousand dollars that you perhaps remember. Which justifies the reflection that some stories, as well as life, and puppies thrown into wells, move around in circles. Painfully but briefly we must shed light on Jacob's words.

The foundation of his fortune was made when he was twenty. A poor coal-digger (ever hear of a rich one?) had saved a dollar or two and bought a small tract of land on a hillside on which he tried to raise corn. Not a nubbin. Jacob, whose nose was a divining-rod, told him there was a vein of coal beneath. He bought the land from the miner for $125 and sold it a month afterward for $10,000. Luckily the miner had enough left of his sale money to drink himself into a black coat opening in the back, as soon as he heard the news.

And so, for forty years afterward, we find Jacob illuminated with the sudden thought that if he could make restitution of this sum of money to the heirs or assigns of the unlucky miner, respite and Nepenthe might be his.

And now must come swift action, for we have here some four thousand words and not a tear shed and never a pistol, joke, safe, nor bottle cracked.

Old Jacob hired a dozen private detectives to find the heirs, if any existed, of the old miner, Hugh McLeod.

Get the point? Of course I know as well as you do that Thomas is going to be the heir. I might have concealed the name; but why always hold back your mystery till the end? I say, let it come near the middle so people can stop reading there if they want to.

After the detectives had trailed false clues about three thousand dollars—I mean miles—they cornered Thomas at the grocery and got his confession that Hugh McLeod had been his grandfather, and that there were no other heirs. They arranged a meeting for him and old Jacob one morning in one of their offices.

Jacob liked the young man very much. He liked the way he looked straight at him when he talked, and the way he threw his bicycle cap over the top of a rose-colored vase on the centre-table.

There was a slight flaw in Jacob's system of restitution. He did not consider that the act, to be perfect, should include confession. So he represented himself to be the agent of the purchaser of the land who had sent him to refund the sale price for the ease of his conscience.

"Well, sir," said Thomas, "this sounds to me like an illustrated post-card from South Boston with 'We're having a good time here' written on it. I don't know the game. Is this ten thousand dollars money, or do I have to save so many coupons to get it?"

Old Jacob counted out to him twenty five-hundred-dollar bills.

That was better, he thought, than a check. Thomas put them thoughtfully into his pocket.

"Grandfather's best thanks," he said, "to the party who sends it."

Jacob talked on, asking him about his work, how he spent his leisure time, and what his ambitions were. The more he saw and heard of Thomas, the better he liked him. He had not met many young men in Bagdad so frank and wholesome.

"I would like to have you visit my house," he said. "I might help you in investing or laying out your money. I am a very wealthy man. I have a daughter about grown, and I would like for you to know her. There are not many young men I would care to have call on her."

"I'm obliged," said Thomas. "I'm not much at making calls. It's generally the side entrance for mine. And, besides, I'm engaged to a girl that has the Delaware peach crop killed in the blossom. She's a parlor maid in a house where I deliver goods. She won't be working there much longer, though. Say, don't forget to give your friend my grandfather's best regards. You'll excuse me now; my wagon's outside with a lot of green stuff that's got to be delivered. See you again, sir."

At eleven Thomas delivered some bunches of parsley and lettuce at the Spraggins mansion. Thomas was only twenty-two; so, as he came back, he took out the handful of five-hundred-dollar bills and waved them carelessly. Annette took a pair of eyes as big as creamed onion to the cook.

"I told you he was a count," she said, after relating. "He never would carry on with me."

"But you say he showed money," said the cook.

"Hundreds of thousands," said Annette. "Carried around loose in his pockets. And he never would look at me."

"It was paid to me to-day," Thomas was explaining to Celia outside. "It came from my grandfather's estate. Say, Cele, what's the use of waiting now? I'm going to quit the job to-night. Why can't we get married next week?"

"Tommy," said Celia. "I'm no parlor maid. I've been fooling you. I'm Miss Spraggins—Celia Spraggins. The newspapers say I'll be worth forty million dollars some day."

Thomas pulled his cap down straight on his head for the first time since we have known him.

"I suppose then," said he, "I suppose then you'll not be marrying me next week. But you *can* whistle."

"No," said Celia, "I'll not be marrying you next week. My father would never let me marry a grocer's clerk. But I'll marry you to-night, Tommy, if you say so."

Old Jacob Spraggins came home at 9:30 P. M., in his motor car. The make of it you will have to surmise sorrowfully; I am giving you unsubsidized fiction; had it been a street car I could have told you its voltage and the number of wheels it had. Jacob called for his daughter; he had bought a ruby necklace for her, and wanted to hear her say what a kind, thoughtful, dear old dad he was.

There was a brief search in the house for her, and then came Annette, glowing with the pure flame of truth and loyalty well mixed with envy and histrionics.

"Oh, sir," said she, wondering if she should kneel, "Miss Celia's just this minute running away out of the side gate with a young man to be married. I couldn't stop her, sir. They went in a cab."

"What young man?" roared old Jacob.

"A millionaire, if you please, sir—a rich nobleman in disguise. He carries his money with him, and the red peppers and the onions was only to blind us, sir. He never did seem to take to me."

Jacob rushed out in time to catch his car. The chauffeur had been delayed by trying to light a cigarette in the wind.

"Here, Gaston, or Mike, or whatever you call yourself, scoot around the corner quicker than blazes and see if you can see a cab. If you do, run it down."

There was a cab in sight a block away. Gaston, or Mike, with his eyes half shut and his mind on his cigarette, picked up the trail, neatly crowded the cab to the curb and pocketed it.

"What t'ell you doin'?" yelled the cabman.

"Pa!" shrieked Celia.

"Grandfather's remorseful friend's agent!" said Thomas. "Wonder what's on his conscience now."

"A thousand thunders," said Gaston, or Mike. "I have no other match."

"Young man," said old Jacob, severely, "how about that parlor maid you were engaged to?"

A couple of years afterward old Jacob went into the office of his private secretary.

"The Amalgamated Missionary Society solicits a contribution of $30,000 toward the conversion of the Koreans," said the secretary.

"Pass 'em up," said Jacob.

"The University of Plumville writes that its yearly endowment fund of $50,000 that you bestowed upon it is past due."

"Tell 'em it's been cut out."

"The Scientific Society of Clam Cove, Long Island, asks for $10,000 to buy alcohol to preserve specimens."

"Waste basket."

"The Society for Providing Healthful Recreation for Working Girls wants $20,000 from you to lay out a golf course."

"Tell 'em to see an undertaker."

"Cut 'em all out," went on Jacob. "I've quit being a good thing. I need every dollar I can scrape or save. I want you to write to the directors of every company that I'm interested in and recommend a 10 per cent. cut in salaries. And say—I noticed half a cake of soap lying in a corner of the hall as I came in. I want you to speak to the scrubwoman about waste. I've got no money to throw away. And say—we've got vinegar pretty well in hand, haven't we?'

"The Globe Spice & Seasons Company," said secretary, "controls the market at present."

"Raise vinegar two cents a gallon. Notify all our branches."

Suddenly Jacob Spraggins's plump red face relaxed into a

pulpy grin. He walked over to the secretary's desk and showed a small red mark on his thick forefinger.

"Bit it," he said, "darned if he didn't, and he ain't had the tooth three weeks—Jaky McLeod, my Celia's kid. He'll be worth a hundred millions by the time he's twenty-one if I can pile it up for him."

As he was leaving, old Jacob turned at the door, and said:

"Better make that vinegar raise three cents instead of two. I'll be back in an hour and sign the letters."

The true history of the Caliph Harun Al Rashid relates that toward the end of his reign he wearied of philanthropy, and caused to be beheaded all his former favorites and companions of his "Arabian Nights" rambles. Happy are we in these days of enlightenment, when the only death warrant the caliphs can serve on us is in the form of a tradesman's bill.

The Girl and the Habit

HABIT—a tendency or aptitude acquired by custom or frequent repetition.

THE critics have assailed every source of inspiration save one. To that one we are driven for our moral theme. When we levied upon the masters of old they gleefully dug up the parallels to our columns. When we strove to set forth real life they reproached us for trying to imitate Henry George, George Washington, Washington Irving, and Irving Bacheller. We wrote of the West and the East, and they accused us of both Jesse and Henry James. We wrote from our heart—and they said something about a disordered liver. We took a text from Matthew or—er—yes, Deuteronomy, but the preachers were hammering away at the inspiration idea before we could get into type. So, driven to the wall, we go for our subject-matter to the reliable, old, moral, unassailable vade mecum—the unabridged dictionary.

Miss Merriam was cashier at Hinkle's. Hinkle's is one of the big downtown restaurants. It is in what the papers call the "financial district." Each day from 12 o'clock to 2 Hinkle's was full of hungry customers—messenger boys, stenographers, brokers, owners of mining stock, promoters, inventors with patents pending—and also people with money.

The cashiership at Hinkle's was no sinecure. Hinkle egged and toasted and griddle-caked and coffeed a good many customers; and he lunched (as good a word as "dined") many more. It might be said that Hinkle's breakfast crowd was a contingent, but his luncheon patronage amounted to a horde.

Miss Merriam sat on a stool at a desk inclosed on three sides by a strong, high fencing of woven brass wire. Through an arched opening at the bottom you thrust your waiter's check and the money, while your heart went pit-a-pat.

For Miss Merriam was lovely and capable. She could take 45 cents out of a $2 bill and refuse an offer of marriage before you could—Next!—lost your chance—please don't shove. She could keep cool and collected while she collected your check, give you the correct change, win your heart, indicate the toothpick stand, and rate you to a quarter of a cent better than Bradstreet could to a thousand in less time than it takes to pepper an egg with one of Hinkle's casters.

There is an old and dignified allusion to the "fierce light that beats upon a throne." The light that beats upon the young lady cashier's cage is also something fierce. The other fellow is responsible for the slang.

Every male patron of Hinkle's, from the A. D. T. boys up to the curbstone brokers, adored Miss Merriam. When they paid their checks they wooed her with every wile known to Cupid's art. Between the meshes of the brass railing went smiles, winks, compliments, tender vows, invitations to dinner, sighs, languishing looks and merry banter that was wafted pointedly back by the gifted Miss Merriam.

There is no coign of vantage more effective than the position of young lady cashier. She sits there, easily queen of the court of commerce; she is duchess of dollars and devoirs, countess of compliments and coin, leading lady of love and luncheon. You take from her a smile and a Canadian dime, and you go your way uncomplaining. You count the cheery word or two that she tosses you as misers count their treasures; and you pocket the change for a five uncomputed. Perhaps the brass-bound inaccessibility multiplies her charms—anyhow, she is a shirt-waisted angel, immaculate, trim, manicured, seductive, bright-eyed, ready, alert—Psyche, Circe, and Ate in one, separating you from your circulating medium after your sirloin medium.

The young men who broke bread at Hinkle's never settled with the cashier without an exchange of badinage and open compliment. Many of them went to greater lengths and dropped promissory hints of theatre tickets and chocolates. The older men spoke plainly of orange blossoms, generally withering the tentative petals by after-allusions to Harlem flats. One broker, who had been squeezed by copper proposed to Miss Merriam more regularly than he ate.

During a brisk luncheon hour Miss Merriam's conversation, while she took money for checks, would run something like this:

"Good morning, Mr. Haskins—sir?—it's natural, thank you—don't be quite so fresh . . . Hello, Johnny—ten, fifteen, twenty—chase along now or they'll take the letters off your cap . . . Beg pardon—count it again, please—Oh, don't mention it . . . Vaudeville?—thanks; not on your moving picture—I was to see Carter in Hedda Gabler on Wednesday night with Mr. Simmons . . . 'Scuse me, I thought that was a quarter . . . Twenty-five and seventy-five's a dollar—got that ham-and-cabbage habit yet. I see, Billy . . . Who are you addressing?—say—you'll get all that's coming to you in a minute . . . Oh, fudge! Mr. Bassett—you're always fooling—no—? Well, maybe I'll marry you some day—three, four and sixty-five is five . . . Kindly keep them remarks to yourself, if you please . . . Ten cents?—'scuse me; the check calls for seventy—well, maybe it is a one instead of a seven . . . Oh, do you like it that way, Mr. Saunders?—some prefer a pomp; but they say this Cleo de Merody does suit refined features . . . and ten is fifty . . . Hike along there, buddy; don't take this for a Coney Island ticket booth . . . Huh?—why, Macy's—don't it fit nice? Oh, no, it isn't too cool—these light-weight fabrics is all the go this season . . . Come again, please—that's the third time you've tried to—what?—forget it—that lead quarter is an old friend of mine . . . Sixty-five?—must have had your salary raised, Mr. Wilson . . . I seen you on Sixth Avenue Tuesday afternoon, Mr. De Forest—swell?—oh, my!—who is she?... What's the matter with it?—why, it ain't money—what?—Columbian half?—well, this ain't South America . . . Yes, I like the mixed best—Friday?—awfully sorry, but I take my jiu-jitsu lesson on Friday—Thursday, then . . . Thanks—that's sixteen times I've been told that this morning—I guess I must be beautiful . . . Cut that out, please—who do you think I am? . . . Why, Mr. Westbrook—do you really think so?—the idea!—one—eighty and twenty's a dollar—thank you ever so much, but I don't ever go automobile riding with gentlemen—your aunt?—well, that's different—perhaps . . . Please don't get fresh—your check was fifteen cents, I believe—kindly step aside and let . . . Hello, Ben—coming around Thursday evening?—there's a gentleman going to send around a box of chocolates, and . . . forty and sixty is a dollar, and one is two..."

About the middle of one afternoon the dizzy goddess Vertigo—whose other name is Fortune—suddenly smote an old, wealthy and eccentric banker while he was walking past Hinkle's, on his way to a street car. A wealthy and eccentric banker who rides in street cars is—move up, please; there are others.

A Samaritan, a Pharisee, a man and a policeman who were first on the spot lifted Banker McRamsey and carried him into Hinkle's restaurant. When the aged but indestructible banker opened his eyes he saw a beautiful vision bending over him with a pitiful, tender smile, bathing his forehead with beef tea and chafing his hands with something frappé out of a chafing-dish. Mr. McRamsey sighed, lost a vest button, gazed with deep gratitude upon his fair preserveress, and then recovered consciousness.

To the Seaside Library all who are anticipating a romance! Banker McRamsey had an aged and respected wife, and his sentiments toward Miss Merriam were fatherly. He talked to her for half an hour with interest—not the kind that went with his talks during business hours. The next day he brought Mrs. McRamsey down to see her. The old couple were childless—they had only a married daughter living in Brooklyn.

To make a short story shorter, the beautiful cashier won the hearts of the good old couple. They came to Hinkle's again and again; they invited her to their old-fashioned but splendid home in one of the East Seventies. Miss Merriam's winning loveliness, her sweet frankness and impulsive heart took them by storm. They said a hundred times that Miss Merriam reminded them so much of their lost daughter. The Brooklyn matron, née Ramsey, had the figure of Buddha and a face like the ideal of an art photographer. Miss Merriam was a combination of curves, smiles, rose leaves, pearls, satin and hair-tonic posters. Enough of the fatuity of parents.

A month after the worthy couple became acquainted with Miss Merriam, she stood before Hinkle one afternoon and resigned her cashiership.

"They're going to adopt me," she told the bereft restaurateur. "They're funny old people, but regular dears. And the swell home they have got! Say, Hinkle, there isn't any use of talking—I'm on the à la carte to wear brown duds and goggles in a whiz wagon, or marry a duke at least. Still, I somehow hate to break out of the old cage. I've been cashiering so long I feel funny doing anything else. I'll miss joshing the fellows awfully when they line up to pay for the buckwheats and. But I can't let this chance slide. And they're awfully good, Hinkle;

I know I'll have a swell time. You owe me nine-sixty-two and a half for the week. Cut out the half if it hurts you, Hinkle."

And they did. Miss Merriam became Miss Rosa McRamsey. And she graced the transition. Beauty is only skin-deep, but the nerves lie very near to the skin. Nerve—but just here will you oblige by perusing again the quotation with which this story begins?

The McRamseys poured out money like domestic champagne to polish their adopted one. Milliners, dancing masters and private tutors got it. Miss—er—McRamsey was grateful, loving, and tried to forget Hinkle's. To give ample credit to the adaptability of the American girl, Hinkle's did fade from her memory and speech most of the time.

Not every one will remember when the Earl of Hitesbury came to East Seventy——Street, America. He was only a fair-to-medium earl, without debts, and he created little excitement. But you will surely remember the evening when the Daughters of Benevolence held their bazaar in the W——f-A——a Hotel. For you were there, and you wrote a note to Fannie on the hotel paper, and mailed it, just to show her that—you did not? Very well; that was the evening the baby was sick, of course.

At the bazaar the McRamseys were prominent. Miss Mer—er—McRamsey was exquisitely beautiful. The Earl of Hitesbury had been very attentive to her since he dropped in to have a look at America. At the charity bazaar the affair was supposed to be going to be pulled off to a finish. An earl is as good as a duke. Better. His standing may be lower, but his outstanding accounts are also lower.

Our ex-young-lady-cashier was assigned to a booth. She was expected to sell worthless articles to nobs and snobs at exorbitant prices. The proceeds of the bazaar were to be used for giving the poor children of the slums a Christmas din——Say! did you ever wonder where they get the other 364?

Miss McRamsey—beautiful, palpitating, excited, charming, radiant—fluttered about in her booth. An imitation brass network, with a little arched opening, fenced her in.

Along came the Earl, assured, delicate, accurate, admiring—admiring greatly, and faced the open wicket.

"You look chawming, you know—'pon my word you do—my deah," he said, beguilingly.

Miss McRamsey whirled around.

"Cut that joshing out," she said, coolly and briskly. "Who do you think you are talking to? Your check, please. Oh, Lordy!—"

Patrons of the bazaar became aware of a commotion and pressed around a certain booth. The Earl of Hitesbury stood near by pulling a pale blond and puzzled whisker.

"Miss McRamsey has fainted," some one explained.

Proof of the Pudding

SPRING winked a vitreous optic at Editor Westbrook of the *Minerva Magazine*, and deflected him from his course. He had lunched in his favorite corner of a Broadway hotel, and was returning to his office when his feet became entangled in the lure of the vernal coquette. Which is by way of saying that he turned eastward in Twenty-sixth Street, safely forded the spring freshet of vehicles in Fifth Avenue, and meandered along the walks of budding Madison Square.

The lenient air and the settings of the little park almost formed a pastoral; the color motif was green—the presiding shade at the creation of man and vegetation.

The callow grass between the walks was the color of verdigris, a poisonous green, reminiscent of the horde of derelict humans that had breathed upon the soil during the summer and autumn. The bursting tree buds looked strangely familiar to those who had botanized among the garnishings of the fish course of a forty-cent dinner. The sky above was of that pale aquamarine tint that ballroom poets rhyme with "true" and "Sue" and "coo." The one natural and frank color visible was the ostensible green of the newly painted benches—a shade between the color of a pickled cucumber and that of a last year's fast-black cravenette raincoat. But, to the city-bred eye of Editor Westbrook, the landscape appeared a masterpiece.

And now, whether you are of those who rush in, or of the gentle concourse that fears to tread, you must follow in a brief invasion of the editor's mind.

Editor Westbrook's spirit was contented and serene. The April number of the *Minerva* had sold its entire edition before the tenth day of the month—a newsdealer in Keokuk had written that he could have sold fifty copies more if he had 'em. The owners of the magazine had raised his (the editor's) salary; he had just installed in his home a jewel of a recently imported cook who was afraid of policemen; and the morning papers had published in full a speech he had made at a publishers' banquet. Also there were echoing in his mind the jubilant notes of a splendid song that his charming young wife had sung to him before he left his up-town apartment that morning. She was taking enthusiastic interest in her music of late, practising early and diligently. When he had complimented her on the improvement in her voice she had fairly hugged him for joy at his praise. He felt, too, the benign, tonic medicament of the trained nurse, Spring, tripping softly adown the wards of the convalescent city.

While Editor Westbrook was sauntering between the rows of park benches (already filling with vagrants and the guardians of lawless childhood) he felt his sleeve grasped and held. Suspecting that he was about to be panhandled, he turned a cold and unprofitable face, and saw that his captor was—Dawe—Shackleford Dawe, dingy, almost ragged, the genteel scarcely visible in him through the deeper lines of the shabby.

While the editor is pulling himself out of his surprise, a flashlight biography of Dawe is offered.

He was a fiction writer, and one of Westbrook's old acquaintances. At one time they might have called each other old friends. Dawe had some money in those days, and lived in a decent apartment house near Westbrook's. The two families often went to theatres and dinners together. Mrs. Dawe and Mrs. Westbrook became "dearest" friends. Then one day a little tentacle of the octopus, just to amuse itself, ingurgitated Dawe's capital, and he moved to the Gramercy Park neighborhood where one, for a few groats per week, may sit upon one's trunk under eight-branched chandeliers and opposite Carrara marble mantels and watch the mice play upon the floor. Dawe thought to live by writing fiction. Now and then he sold a story. He submitted many to Westbrook. The *Minerva* printed one or two of them; the rest were returned. Westbrook sent a careful and conscientious personal letter with each rejected manuscript, pointing out in detail his reasons for considering it unavailable. Editor Westbrook had his own clear conception of what constituted good fiction. So had Dawe. Mrs. Dawe was mainly concerned about the constituents of the scanty dishes of food that she managed to scrape together. One day Dawe had been spouting to her about the excellencies of certain French writers. At dinner they sat down to a dish that a hungry schoolboy could have encompassed at a gulp. Dawe commented.

"It's Maupassant hash," said Mrs. Dawe. "It may not be art, but I do wish you would do a five-course Marion Crawford serial with an Ella Wheeler Wilcox sonnet for dessert. I'm hungry."

As far as this from success was Shackleford Dawe when he plucked Editor Westbrook's sleeve in Madison Square. That was the first time the editor had seen Dawe in several months.

"Why, Shack, is this you?" said Westbrook, somewhat awkwardly, for the form of his phrase seemed to touch upon the other's changed appearance.

"Sit down for a minute," said Dawe, tugging at his sleeve. "This is my office. I can't come to yours, looking as I do. Oh, sit down—you won't be disgraced. Those half-plucked birds on the other benches will take you for a swell porch-climber. They won't know you are only an editor."

"Smoke, Shack?" said Editor Westbrook, sinking cautiously upon the virulent green bench. He always yielded gracefully when he did yield.

Dawe snapped at the cigar as a kingfisher darts at a sun-perch, or a girl pecks at a chocolate cream.

"I have just—" began the editor.

"Oh, I know; don't finish," said Dawe. "Give me a match. You have just ten minutes to spare. How did you manage to get past my office-boy and invade my sanctum? There he goes now, throwing his club at a dog that couldn't read the 'Keep off the Grass' signs."

"How goes the writing?" asked the editor. "Look at me," said Dawe, "for your answer. Now don't put on that embarrassed, friendly-but-honest look and ask me why I don't get a job as a wine agent or a cab driver. I'm in the fight to a finish. I know I can write good fiction and I'll force you fellows to admit it yet. I'll make you change the spelling of 'regrets' to 'c-h-e-q-u-e' before I'm done with you."

Editor Westbrook gazed through his nose-glasses with a sweetly sorrowful, omniscient, sympathetic, skeptical expression—the copyrighted expression of the editor beleagured by the unavailable contributor.

"Have you read the last story I sent you—'The Alarum of the Soul'?" asked Dawe.

"Carefully. I hesitated over that story, Shack, really I did. It had some good points. I was writing you a letter to send with it when it goes back to you. I regret—"

"Never mind the regrets," said Dawe, grimly. "There's neither salve nor sting in 'em any more. What I want to know is *why*. Come now; out with the good points first."

"The story," said Westbrook, deliberately, after a suppressed sigh, "is written around an almost original plot. Characterization—the best you have done. Construction—almost as good, except for a few weak joints which might be strengthened by a few changes and touches. It was a good story, except—"

"I can write English, can't I?" interrupted Dawe.

"I have always told you," said the editor, "that you had a style."

"Then the trouble is—"

"Same old thing," said Editor Westbrook. "You work up to your climax like an artist. And then you turn yourself into a photographer. I don't know what form of obstinate madness possesses you, but that is what you do with everything that you write. No, I will retract the comparison with the photographer. Now and then photography, in spite of its impossible perspective, manages to record a fleeting glimpse of truth. But you spoil every dénouement by those flat, drab, obliterating strokes of your brush that I have so often complained of. If you would rise to the literary pinnacle of your dramatic senses, and paint them in the high colors that art requires, the postman would leave fewer bulky, self-addressed envelopes at your door."

"Oh, fiddles and footlights!" cried Dawe, derisively. "You've got that old sawmill drama kink in your brain yet. When the man with the black mustache kidnaps golden-haired Bessie you are bound to have the mother kneel and raise her hands in the spotlight and say: 'May high heaven witness that I will rest neither night nor day till the heartless villain that has stolen me child feels the weight of another's vengeance!'"

Editor Westbrook conceded a smile of impervious complacency.

"I think," said he, "that in real life the woman would express herself in those words or in very similar ones."

"Not in a six hundred nights' run anywhere but on the stage," said Dawe hotly. "I'll tell you what she'd say in real life. She'd say: 'What! Bessie led away by a strange man? Good Lord! It's one trouble after another! Get my other hat, I must hurry around to the police-station. Why wasn't somebody looking after her, I'd like to know? For God's sake, get out of my way or I'll never get ready. Not that hat—the brown one with the velvet bows. Bessie must have been crazy; she's usually shy of strangers. Is that too much powder? Lordy! How I'm upset!'

"That's the way she'd talk," continued Dawe. "People in real life don't fly into heroics and blank verse at emotional crises. They simply can't do it. If they talk at all on such occasions they draw from the same vocabulary that they use every day, and muddle up their words and ideas a little more, that's all."

"Shack," said Editor Westbrook impressively, "did you ever pick up the mangled and lifeless form of a child from under the fender of a street car, and carry it in your arms and lay it down before the distracted mother? Did you ever do that and listen to the words of grief and despair as they flowed spontaneously from her lips?"

"I never did," said Dawe. "Did you?"

"Well, no," said Editor Westbrook, with a slight frown. "But I can well imagine what she would say."

"So can I," said Dawe.

And now the fitting time had come for Editor Westbrook to play the oracle and silence his opinionated contributor. It was not for an unarrived fictionist to dictate words to be uttered by the heroes and heroines of the *Minerva Magazine*, contrary to the theories of the editor thereof.

"My dear Shack," said he, "if I know anything of life I know that every sudden, deep and tragic emotion in the human heart calls forth an apposite, concordant, conformable and proportionate expression of feeling. How much of this inevitable accord between expression and feeling should be attributed to nature, and how much to the influence of art, it would be difficult to say. The sublimely terrible roar of the lioness that has been deprived of her cubs is dramatically as far above her customary whine and purr as the kingly and transcendent utterances of Lear are above the level of his senile vaporings. But it is also true that all men and women have what may be called a sub-conscious dramatic sense that is awakened by a sufficiently deep and powerful emotion—a sense unconsciously acquired from literature and the stage that prompts them to express those emotions in language befitting their importance and histrionic value."

"And in the name of the seven sacred saddle-blankets of Sagittarius, where did the stage and literature get the stunt?" asked Dawe.

"From life," answered the editor, triumphantly.

The story writer rose from the bench and gesticulated eloquently but dumbly. He was beggared for words with which to formulate adequately his dissent.

On a bench nearby a frowzy loafer opened his red eyes and perceived that his moral support was due a downtrodden brother.

"Punch him one, Jack," he called hoarsely to Dawe. "W'at's he come makin' a noise like a penny arcade for amongst gen'lemen that comes in the square to set and think?"

Editor Westbrook looked at his watch with an affected show of leisure.

"Tell me," asked Dawe, with truculent anxiety, "what especial faults in 'The Alarum of the Soul' caused you to throw it down?"

"When Gabriel Murray," said Westbrook, "goes to his telephone and is told that his fiancée has been shot by a burglar, he says—I do not recall the exact words, but—"

"I do," said Dawe. "He says: 'Damn Central; she always cuts me off.' (And then to his friend) 'Say, Tommy, does a thirty-two bullet make a big hole? It's kind of hard luck, ain't it? Could you get me a drink from the sideboard, Tommy? No; straight; nothing on the side.'"

"And again," continued the editor, without pausing for argument, "when Berenice opens the letter from her husband informing her that he has fled with the manicure girl, her words are—let me see—"

"She says," interposed the author: "'Well, what do you think of that!'"

"Absurdly inappropriate words," said Westbrook, "presenting an anti-climax—plunging the story into hopeless bathos. Worse yet; they mirror life falsely. No human being ever uttered banal colloquialisms when confronted by sudden tragedy."

"Wrong," said Dawe, closing his unshaven jaws doggedly. "I say no man or woman ever spouts 'high-falutin' talk when they go up against a real climax. They talk naturally and a little worse."

The editor rose from the bench with his air of indulgence and inside information.

"Say, Westbrook," said Dawe, pinning him by the lapel, "would you have accepted 'The Alarum of the Soul' if you had believed that the actions and words of the characters were true to life in the parts of the story that we discussed?"

"It is very likely that I would, if I believed that way," said the editor. "But I have explained to you that I do not."

"If I could prove to you that I am right?"

"I'm sorry, Shack, but I'm afraid I haven't time to argue any further just now."

"I don't want to argue," said Dawe. "I want to demonstrate to you from life itself that my view is the correct one."

"How could you do that?" asked Westbrook, in a surprised tone.

"Listen," said the writer, seriously. "I have thought of a way.

It is important to me that my theory of true-to-life fiction be recognized as correct by the magazines. I've fought for it for three years, and I'm down to my last dollar, with two months' rent due."

"I have applied the opposite of your theory," said the editor, "in selecting the fiction for the *Minerva Magazine*. The circulation has gone up from ninety thousand to—"

"Four hundred thousand," said Dawe. "Whereas it should have been boosted to a million."

"You said something to me just now about demonstrating your pet theory."

"I will. If you'll give me about half an hour of your time I'll prove to you that I am right. I'll prove it by Louise."

"Your wife!" exclaimed Westbrook. "How?"

"Well, not exactly by her, but *with* her," said Dawe. "Now, you know how devoted and loving Louise has always been. She thinks I'm the only genuine preparation on the market that bears the old doctor's signature. She's been fonder and more faithful than ever, since I've been cast for the neglected genius part."

"Indeed, she is a charming and admirable life companion," agreed the editor. "I remember what inseparable friends she and Mrs. Westbrook once were. We are both lucky chaps, Shack, to have such wives. You must bring Mrs. Dawe up some evening soon, and we'll have one of those informal chafing-dish suppers that we used to enjoy so much."

"Later," said Dawe. "When I get another shirt. And now I'll tell you my scheme. When I was about to leave home after breakfast—if you can call tea and oatmeal breakfast—Louise told me she was going to visit her aunt in Eighty-ninth Street. She said she would return at three o'clock. She is always on time to a minute. It is now—"

Dawe glanced toward the editor's watch pocket.

"Twenty-seven minutes to three," said Westbrook, scanning his time-piece.

"We have just enough time," said Dawe. "We will go to my flat at once. I will write a note, address it to her and leave it on the table where she will see it as she enters the door. You and I will be in the dining-room concealed by the portières. In that note I'll say that I have fled from her forever with an affinity who understands the needs of my artistic soul as she never did. When she reads it we will observe her actions and hear her words. Then we will know which theory is the correct one—yours or mine."

"Oh, never!" exclaimed the editor, shaking his head. "That would be inexcusably cruel. I could not consent to have Mrs. Dawe's feelings played upon in such a manner."

"Brace up," said the writer. "I guess I think as much of her as you do. It's for her benefit as well as mine. I've got to get a market for my stories in some way. It won't hurt Louise. She's healthy and sound. Her heart goes as strong as a ninety-eight-cent watch. It'll last for only a minute, and then I'll step out and explain to her. You really owe it to me to give me the chance, Westbrook."

Editor Westbrook at length yielded, though but half willingly. And in the half of him that consented lurked the vivisectionist that is in all of us. Let him who has not used the scalpel rise and stand in his place. Pity 'tis that there are not enough rabbits and guinea-pigs to go around.

The two experimenters in Art left the Square and hurried eastward and then to the south until they arrived in the Gramercy neighborhood. Within its high iron railings the little park had put on its smart coat of vernal green, and was admiring itself in its fountain mirror. Outside the railings the hollow square of crumbling houses, shells of a bygone gentry, leaned as if in ghostly gossip over the forgotten doings of the vanished quality. *Sic transit gloria urbis.*

A block or two north of the Park, Dawe steered the editor again eastward, then, after covering a short distance, into a lofty but narrow flathouse burdened with a floridly over-decorated façade. To the fifth story they toiled, and Dawe, panting, pushed his latch-key into the door of one of the front flats.

When the door opened Editor Westbrook saw, with feelings of pity, how meanly and meagerly the rooms were furnished.

"Get a chair, if you can find one," said Dawe, "while I hunt up pen and ink. Hello, what's this? Here's a note from Louise. She must have left it there when she went out this morning."

He picked up an envelope that lay on the centre-table and tore it open. He began to read the letter that he drew out of it; and once having begun it aloud he so read it through to the end. These are the words that Editor Westbrook heard:

"DEAR SHACKLEFORD:

"By the time you get this I will be about a hundred miles away and still a-going. I've got a place in the chorus of the Occidental Opera Co., and we start on the road to-day at twelve o'clock. I didn't want to starve to death, and so I decided to make my own living. I'm not coming back. Mrs. Westbrook is going with me. She said she was tired of living with a combination phonograph, iceberg and dictionary, and she's not coming back, either. We've been practising the songs and dances for two months on the quiet. I hope you will be successful, and get along all right! Good-bye.

"LOUISE."

Dawe dropped the letter, covered his face with his trembling hands, and cried out in a deep, vibrating voice:

"My God, why hast thou given me this cup to drink? Since she is false, then let Thy Heaven's fairest gifts, faith and love, become the jesting by-words of traitors and fiends!"

Editor Westbrook's glasses fell to the floor. The fingers of one hand fumbled with a button on his coat as he blurted between his pale lips:

"Say, Shack, ain't that a hell of a note? Wouldn't that knock you off your perch, Shack? Ain't it hell, now, Shack—ain't it?"

A NOTE ON LITERATURE

LITERATURE, like any other art, is singularly interesting to the artist; and, in a degree peculiar to itself among the arts, it is useful to mankind. These are the sufficient justifications for any young man or woman who adopts it as the business of his life. I shall not say much about the wages. A writer can live by his writing. If not so luxuriously as by other trades, then less luxuriously. The nature of the work he does all day will more affect his happiness than the quality of his dinner at night. Whatever be your calling, and however much it brings you in the year, you could still, you know, get more by cheating. We all suffer ourselves to be too much concerned about a little poverty; but such considerations should not move us in the choice of that which is to be the business and justification of so great a portion of our lives; and like the missionary, the patriot, or the philosopher, we should all choose that poor and brave career in which we can do the most and best for mankind. Now Nature, faithfully followed, proves herself a careful mother. A lad, for some liking to the jingle of words, betakes himself to letters for his life; by-and-by, when he learns more gravity, he finds that he has chosen better than he knew; that if he earns little, he is earning it amply; that if he receives a small wage, he is in a position to do considerable services; that it is in his power, in some small measure, to protect the oppressed and to defend the truth. So kindly is the world arranged, such great profit may arise from a small degree of human reliance on oneself, and such, in particular, is the happy star of this trade of writing, that it should combine pleasure and profit to both parties, and be at once agreeable, like fiddling, and useful, like good preaching.

• • • • • • •

Man is imperfect; yet, in his literature, he must express himself and his own views and preferences; for to do anything else is to do a far more perilous thing than to risk being immoral: it is to be sure of being untrue. To ape a sentiment, even a good one, is to travesty a sentiment; that will not be helpful. To conceal a sentiment, if you are sure you hold it, is to take a liberty with truth. There is probably no point of view possible to a sane man but contains some truth and, in the true connection, might be profitable to the race. I am not afraid of the truth, if any one could tell it me, but I am afraid of parts of it impertinently uttered. There is a time to dance and a time to mourn; to be harsh as well as to be sentimental; to be ascetic as well as to glorify the appetites; and if a man were to combine all these extremes into his work, each in its place and proportion, that work would be the world's masterpiece of morality as well as of art. Partiality is immorality; for any book is wrong that gives a misleading picture of the world and life. The trouble is that the weakling must be partial; the work of one proving dank and depressing; of another, cheap and vulgar; of a third, epileptically sensual; of a fourth, sourly ascetic. In literature as in conduct, you can never hope to do exactly right. All you can do is to make as sure as possible; and for that there is but one rule. Nothing should be done in a hurry that can be done slowly. It is no use to write a book and put it by for nine or even ninety years; for in the writing you will have partly convinced yourself; the delay must precede any beginning; and if you meditate a work of art, you should first long roll the subject under the tongue to make sure you like the flavour, before you brew a volume that shall taste of it from end to end; or if you propose to enter on the field of controversy, you should first have thought upon the question under all conditions, in health as well as in sickness, in sorrow as well as in joy. It is this nearness of examination necessary for any true and kind writing, that makes the practice of the art a prolonged and noble education for the writer.

GEOFFREY CHAUCER

BEN JONSON

SIR PHILLIP SIDNEY

EDMUND SPENSER

There is plenty to do, plenty to say, or to say over again, in the meantime. Any literary work which conveys faithful facts or pleasing impressions is a service to the public. It is even a service to be thankfully proud of having rendered. The slightest novels are a blessing to those in distress, not chloroform itself a greater. Our fine old sea-captain's life was justified when Carlyle soothed his mind with *The King's Own* or *Newton Forster.* To please is to serve; and so far from its being difficult to instruct while you amuse, it is difficult to do the one thoroughly without the other. Some part of the writer or his life will crop out in even a vapid book; and to read a novel that was conceived with any force is to multiply experience and to exercise the sympathies.

JOHN DRYDEN

FRANCIS BACON

JOSEPH ADDISON

JONATHAN SWIFT

Every article, every piece of verse, every essay, every *entre-filet*, is destined to pass, however swiftly, through the minds of some portion of the public, and to colour, however transiently, their thoughts. When any subject falls to be discussed, some scribbler on a paper has the invaluable opportunity of beginning its discussion in a dignified and human spirit; and if there were enough who did so in our public press, neither the public nor the Parliament would find it in their minds to drop to meaner thoughts. The writer has the chance to stumble, by the way, on something pleasing, something interesting, something encouraging, were it only to a single reader.

He will be unfortunate, indeed, if he suit no one. He has the chance, besides, to stumble on something that a dull person shall be able to comprehend; and for a dull person to have read anything and, for that once, comprehended it, makes a marking epoch in his education.

SAMUEL JOHNSON

OLIVER GOLDSMITH

CHARLES DICKENS

THOMAS CARLYLE

Here, then, is work worth doing and worth trying to do well. And so, if I were minded to welcome any great accession to our trade, it should not be from any reason of a higher wage, but because it was a trade which was useful in a very great and in a very high degree; which every honest tradesman could make more serviceable to mankind in his single strength; which was difficult to do well and possible to do better every year; which called for scrupulous thought on the part of all who practised it, and hence became a perpetual education to their nobler natures; and which, pay it as you please, in the large majority of the best cases will still be underpaid. For surely, at this time of day in the nineteenth century, there is nothing that an honest man should fear more timorously than getting and spending more than he deserves.

. . . .

The most influential books, and the truest in their influence, are works of fiction. They do not pin the reader to a dogma, which he must afterwards discover to be inexact; they do not teach him a lesson, which he must afterwards unlearn. They repeat, they rearrange, they clarify the lessons of life; they disengage us from ourselves, they constrain us to the acquaintance of others; and they show us the web of experience, not as we can see it for ourselves, but with a singular change—that monstrous, consuming *ego* of ours being, for the nonce, struck out. To be so, they must be reasonably true to the human comedy; and any work that is so serves the turn of instruction. But the course of our education is answered best by those poems and romances where we breathe a magnanimous atmosphere of thought and meet generous and pious characters.

WM. M. THACKERAY

GEORGE ELIOT

Excerpt from *Essays in the Art of Writing* by R. L. Stevenson.

Made in United States
Orlando, FL
10 December 2024

55341889R00071